PRAISE FOR SIN SORACCO

"Sin Soracco's let-it-whip style offers no apologies or excuses. . . . *Low Bite* gets everybody in everybody else's faces. . . . fetching twistedness." —*Village Voice*

"*Edge City* is dark and sultry. . . . The author creates an illuminating view of hell as a nightclub that never closes, and there's fire in her portraits of the damned souls who inhabit her apocalyptic world."
—*New York Times Book Review*

"Sin Soracco cooks! Her writing is beyond hip—it struts and whistles down the last dark mile."
—Barry Gifford, author of *Wild at Heart*

SIN SORACCO is the author of *Edge City* (Plume).
She lives in San Francisco.

LOW BITE

BITE

by

Sin Soracco

A PLUME BOOK

PLUME
Published by the Penguin Group
Penguin Books USA Inc., 375 Hudson Street, New York, New York 10014, U.S.A.
Penguin Books Ltd, 27 Wrights Lane, London W8 5TZ, England
Penguin Books Australia Ltd, Ringwood, Victoria, Australia
Penguin Books Canada Ltd, 10 Alcorn Avenue, Toronto, Ontario, Canada M4V 3B2
Penguin Books (N.Z.) Ltd, 182–190 Wairau Road, Auckland 10, New Zealand

Penguin Books Ltd, Registered Offices: Harmondsworth, Middlesex, England

Published by Plume, an imprint of Dutton Signet,
a division of Penguin Books USA Inc.
Originally published in a Black Lizard Books hardcover edition.

First Plume Printing, August, 1994
10 9 8 7 6 5 4 3 2 1

 REGISTERED TRADEMARK—MARCA REGISTRADA

LIBRARY OF CONGRESS CATALOGING-IN-PUBLICATION DATA
Soracco, Sin, 1947–
    Low bite / by Sin Soracco.
        p.   cm.
    ISBN 0-452-27144-4
    1. Prisoners—Fiction.   I. Title.
    [PS3569.0667L6   1994]
    813'.54—dc20   93–44123
                                                    CIP

Printed in the United States of America

PUBLISHER'S NOTE
This is a work of fiction. Names, characters, places, and incidents either are the
product of the author's imagination or are used fictitiously, and any resemblance to
actual persons, living or dead, events, or locales is entirely coincidental.

LOW BITE

• ONE •

The first shot went wild.

Thin and sharp as barbwire, bleached as an old bone, Lily kept climbing the chain-link fence. State issue blanket tied around her waist, state issue gloves covering her hands, up and up she went, her pale hair ribboning in the wind. She knew the fog would hide her until she was over the top. And away.

She stretched the blanket over the razor wire, pressing her weight on it delicately, twisting to see the highway.

The second shot ripped her off the fence. She hit the dirt running zigzag through the winter bare field at the edge of the prison yard, bent double aiming for some nonexistent shelter.

She collapsed with a small scream, her ankle snapped clean from a final misstep into the abandoned weasel burrow.

The guard came up on her cautiously, nervous pistol drawn.

She didn't look at him, just tipped her head back and howled her rage at the sky.

■   ■   ■

The next day Johnson, a sweaty new guard, escorted me past the red brick housing units to the law library for my afternoon shift. I noticed her uniform was tailored so tight her face ballooned strangely from the starched collar of her beige shirt. I didn't mention her missing neck because I wasn't feeling so good about myself, a result of representing Lily in that morning's conferences with the administration.

I leaned over, whispering, "I've got a knife." Stepped out briskly.

Officer Johnson hustled to catch up. "What did you say?"

"Ai! What a night."

She tried to step in front of me. "That's not what you said."

I slid primly around the panting guard. "I whored all night."

"What did you say? Stop! I got to escort you!"

I looked back at her over my shoulder. "Said, 'Snored all night.'"

Johnson squinted her eyes, hustled to catch up. "Are you trying to provoke me, young lady?"

I stopped dead, Johnson ran up over my heels. I didn't remark on it, I'm a tolerant sort of person. "Me? Provoke you? Oh come on."

I watched with detached professional interest as Officer Johnson fumbled with the lock on the law library door. She stepped into the tiny windowless room first, probing for something amiss among the book-lined clutter.

Johnson was always bitching about the law library, how it was a major cause of trouble, no good ever came from it. She started up again, "Makes you think you got rights, as if you were somebody. You people aren't special." She paused for effect. "Just nasty thieving murdering bitches. Devious."

"Dykes." I knew she didn't like dykes. Unnatural.

She didn't quite look at me. "Morgan! I expect this place to be tidy and clean when I come back for count. You never see a broom or what?" She shut her mouth so tight she swallowed her lips.

"Sure thing, Johnson. Sure thing."

I'd already turned away from her to dig my way

through a tower of grimy files. I moved volumes stuffed with papers from the tables to the chairs, others from the shelves to start new piles on the tables. The floor, every flat surface, was littered with crumpled papers, cigarette butts, law books with torn pieces of paper sticking out; my typewriter held a typed sheet, the second draft of an appeal, covered by untidy green inked corrections. Between my successful cases the layers of chaos built up. There weren't many successes.

Prison time is chicken bones, something to be sucked clean. Time is a thing, abstract, made of interlocking gears, everything connected. I scowled at the mess. My notes on a couple of sadly inadequate habeas corpus writs were mixed in with the divorce papers for half the women in general population. The newest craze.

Officer Johnson stood on one foot, then the other, trying to demand more of a commitment. Ignored, she huffed out the door, muttering pointlessly that she'd be back.

Everyone would be back. I wondered how much longer Johnson would last. What sort of shit she'd stir up before her inevitable departure. The possibilities were staggering. I pulled my coffee cup out of the lowest drawer of my desk, filled it from the hooch jar, took a long necessary swallow.

Prison exists to serve one purpose: locking people away from life's good things, usually other people's good things. A temporary solution at best. The combat continues unabated behind the walls. A regular knock-down drag-out with the administration and the guards in here whaling away just like the convicts. Everybody fighting over the good things no one ever gets enough of.

I sat there after Johnson left, counting cigarettes, trying to figure out what my next move should be. So far I'd managed to make a royal mess of things.

I had been convicted of nighttime residential burglary with (unproven) use of force. The DA elaborated, fancifully, I thought, how no one could have gotten by that particular citizen's massive security apparatus or into his expensive new safe without force. The judge gave me four years. So much for independent thinking in the judiciary. Four years. The courts have no appreciation of my skills. Probably a good thing.

I didn't consider that job exactly a failure, more like an embarrassment. I usually worked alone, did my own research, my own setup—just that once I went along as backup on someone else's job. Little things just clog up the works sometimes. I try not to take it personally.

Wearing cascades of Spanish lace, tinkling bracelets, tight black jeans, China swiveled her way into the law library, clicked her tongue and unceremoniously dumped a stack of books off a chair. "Got to get some discipline to your habits, girl." Her voice was musical, seductive.

I moved my eyes a fraction of an inch to look at the newest pile on the floor, back to her. I wasn't thrilled to see her.

China had a warm brown triangular face, full lips, great slanted eyes, a long mane of black hair, and a heart of endless larceny. "You know that guard woulda killed 'er if she was anythin' but a ver' white girl. Crazy gavacha, tryin' to escape like that."

I, like all of us, tell lies and still sleep pretty well. "Lily wasn't tryin' to escape."

"Sure she was."

"Nope." I ruined my morning in conference with the administration about just that thing. Reality can be bought or sold in prison. It's strictly a futures market. We decided, the administration and I, that Lily hadn't been escaping, the guard hadn't shot at her. Those things made unnecessary complications under the circumstances.

Lily never did anything right, poor kid still got cards from the bastard she tried to kill. Postmarked Reno, Las Vegas, Atlantic City: "Havin a wonderful time girl. Placed some bets for you—you always lose. Hahaha."

"I be glad when he's finally dead," she said, "even if it ain't me what does it."

If Lily was charged with escape she would become a

three-time loser: attempted escape, aggravating a guard into using his weapon, the commission of a felony in the course of which bodily injury occurred, her own, but that was just the way things went for her. Other charges could be arranged. Time piled up on time; once it's started there's no way to stop the process, as if punishment feeds on itself growing bloated obese succulent.

I'd made a couple suggestions at the hearing this morning. Only thing the administration and I ever agreed on. Gave me serious doubts about myself. "It's a bad time to be shooting women, you know. This a model prison here."

"Say what?"

I didn't want to go over it. "They aren't filing escape charges against Lily."

"So? The asshole shot at her. She broke her damn ankle. Why don't you file against him for her? You gone let that guard get away with it?"

"Get away with what? Takin' a shot at some broad climbing on the fence? The man be doin' his job."

"No he ain't. Oh no he ain't. We ain't no live targets here."

I stared at the books lining the walls, floor to ceiling, spread around the tables the chairs the floor; not an answer in a one of them. I was at a loss for answers, not a new experience, but the magnitude of my present ignorance appalled me. No wonder the classification officers let me work in the law library so willingly: I hadn't the smallest idea how to do any of the things that needed to be done.

I struggled for equilibrium, frustrated. I was searching for something to ease my thoughts, open my mind to the flow, like a fisherman coaxing a fish in the currents. I took pride in my small catches. But no fish were biting.

I pointed with my cigarette, inadequate. "You know how many cases get heard in court on these things? Exactly none." China still wasn't satisfied. "We ain't goin' to court because there's nothing to it. It never happened. No escape attempt. No shooting."

China sat there unmoving, waiting me out.

"They put Lily back in the nut ward." I lit another cigarette from the butt of the first one, tried once again. "Actually, she put herself there. Damn. Nothin' nobody can do."

"Nothin'?"

"Look, China, this isn't doing you any good. Stay out of it. It's none of yours."

"I just found out she knew him, you know?"

"Who?"

"Lily knew him. My husband. She knew he was rotten, rotten to the core."

"Great. Nice you found someone to support you in that. You still can't get her out from under this one no matter how much you both agree Roland was an asshole."

I never knew what China had in mind, sometimes I wasn't sure China had anything at all on her mind, but I didn't care, she was soothing to look at. "You got to realize that even if the police do find whoever killed your husband it won't shorten your time by one bloody day."

"I hear you, Morgan. But I was hoping maybe Lily—well, I guess it's gone beyond that now. I got to find who killed him on my own." She looked out of the corners of those wondrous eyes, pulling me into her charmed circle. "It's gone way beyond doin' this time. Beyond this funky prison, beyond justice—ain't none of that."

"A matter of money."

"Right in one. He was collecting big that night." Close. Confidential. Candid. "Morgan, listen, there was an easy forty thousand dollars." China paused. It sounded like a nice round sum to me. "Seem like no one have it now though."

I blew smoke rings the way Narcisse the Silent taught me. Buying time. I hadn't seen three inches of money in years.

China smiled, her smooth oval face confident. "That is, don't no one have it but his killer. I want it. You can help me get it."

I didn't fall over dead. Second mistake of the day. Third, if you count teasing Officer Johnson.

■   ■   ■

Old Norah was one of those jailhouse legends, make a hit, then vanish; the cop who chased her coast to coast for ten years finally busted her for torching a hotel to cover her last job. I don't know why we were impressed with that sort of thing, but there might be something to be said for thoroughness. No one ever figured out which one of those eleven corpses was her target.

She seldom talked to the rest of us, just walked the perimeter fence, a pigeon-chested old Italian woman doing her holiday shopping: a prosciutto bone for soup perhaps, a nice chubby salami. She found that weasel burrow out by the fence, squatted patiently in the scrub until one of the babies ventured out, then she snatched it quicker than an ordinary old woman could, big fast hands, zip into the pocket of her faded housecoat.

Alone in the solemnity of her cell, she dedicated her victim to the nameless gods that lived before Latin. She held the trembling creature, her thick fingers pressed on its windpipe in a lock-bone grip.

Then she snapped its neck.

■   ■   ■

When Lily's ankle healed and she finally admitted that she must have been crazy to be walking around in the fog at that time of the morning, they let her back into general population. By that time she was Thorazine-fat, one-thought-bitter: Old Norah was personally and solely responsible for everything that had gone wrong in her life.

Lily shuffled around sort of smiling, planning her next assault. On the fence. On Old Norah. On herself. Promising to set things right. There be time enough.

"I woulda got over if I'da known how to get over but even though I know how now I didn't know how then so I couldna done it. Right? Even if I woulda done it. And I woulda. Let me tell you. But I didn' do it. Now."

I recognized it. Happened to everyone after awhile, talking to hear the sounds pour out.

Lily said to me, "You know you're finished when there's more behind in life than in front." She'd slap her Thorazine ass, laugh high and sad.

Dislocations of minds and bodies start from little shifts: the straight four four of prison time and the internal rhythm of convict time start to conflict. Right at the edge of perception. Bellies pushed forward, women in thong sandals slipped like fish up the green corridors: looking gooooood mamma. Hey mamma and your red-hot mamma smile, can you do it for me, can you walk another mile? Swing those hips. Dance back and forth in your exotic robes, reeking of mail-order perfume, curling irons and gloom, Dixie Peach bleach, stale cigarettes; check it out mamma, got to get it got to get it got to get it move so smooth you can barely see the hand snatch for it.

How it is.

Women with clipped wings, sitting, just staring, hearing but no longer listening, chirping about the streets and how it is. How one day always follows one day.

I was bloody sick of it.

Locked up with liars. Screamers, schemers. Deceivers.

• TWO •

When someone over in the administration building called for a couple hamburgers no mustard ketchup on the fries three strawberry shakes, no one bothered to search the pale idiot-eyed delivery girl.

The police thought of Narcisse the Silent, when they thought about her at all, simply as the deaf and dumb woman who worked in the officers' canteen; she had been chosen for the job because she couldn't hear, kept on when they discovered she was a quick creative fry cook.

Narcisse the Silent was no longer young but she had a lightness that served, a glint of something sly, funny. Between burgers she kept an eye on things, most often the police's things. They never looked behind her blank expression, but then they weren't supposed to. They didn't realize that Narcisse' could hide a four-head VCR on her person, slide past a metal detector, go back for the camera if she had the mood. Our cell was very comfortable.

When we talked she could be as animated as a dancer, her body expressing what feeble vocal chords never could. I was learning to finger sign, still awkward, but I was getting better. Sometimes trying to communicate with her was the single thing that kept me sane.

It was a lazy taste for luxury that put her in prison, she said, her long hands caressing the words, "Lapis lazuli, fire agates, South American emeralds. I loved them, the rich glitter. Didn't even set them in jewelry—"

I understood that. A set stone brought more money, but it was easy to identify.

She shook her head at me, understanding my incorrect agreement. "No. I just loved the stones themselves, I even wanted to learn gem-cutting, but no one would teach me." She touched her useless ears, shrugged. "My interest in drugs just sort of happened. Incidental. Accidental. Not important. You know."

Even her drug use wasn't ordinary. A lot of addicts have a fascination with the needle, but I never saw her doing the blood-balancing ritual in/out with the dropper; she preferred to fall into the arms of Morpheus with tea. She melted down that black tar, adding hot water and lemon as it started to fragment, then transfixed, she sipped on the strange amber liquid, swaying, latched onto some bright elsewhere road undistracted by the noisy everyday after day.

I wondered if this was Narcisse's own music, soundless, a drug like pure mathematics—rhythm, color? Maybe the way she thought was itself different, wordless. Loaded. Whatever it was, it worked well for her. Stubborn, generous, seeming wise beyond her time, she was remarkably content, even in jail. A placid floating junkie Buddha.

Then again, perhaps she was so serene because she was deaf and loaded all the time. Simply couldn't hear the racket.

It all got away from me at about that point. I noticed a lot of things getting away from me, I tried not to mind, failure is the common language of prison.

Around the middle of November I needed to send someone with a message up to Narcisse in the officers' canteen. Old Norah could slither half invisible anywhere on the prison grounds, but I knew that when she'd finally get to the canteen, her mind centered on salami and cheese on rye, she'd forget her errand in the thrill of sandwich dreaming. Narcisse would remind her.

Narcisse reached for her cleaver, waggled the blade in a cheery fashion at Old Norah. Narcisse didn't let anyone, convict or police, be grabbing out whatever they felt like from her kitchen.

Old Norah pretended not to notice, turning away from the sandwich counter she wrapped her dreams in the spittle of her secret language; she fished in her grimy pockets, handed Narcisse my kite.

Narcisse flicked a glance around; nodding briefly she passed Norah a hard-boiled egg. Payment enough. The old woman couldn't read. Narcisse couldn't talk. The privacy of the mails must be protected: I needed two number-ten cans of peaches, another five pounds of sugar. Immediately.

■   ■   ■

Thea and Queenie slipped into the law library with the supplies. Fearless barbarians, pragmatic, cheerfully psychotic, inseparably joined at the hip, they interacted with the rest of us only for their own evil entertainment. They made bad attitude an art.

Thea was a short black-gold woman with a round smiling face that was usually surrounded by dark sculptured curls. That day her newly bleached hair stuck up in bright red spikes at all angles, Afro Punk. I decided not to comment.

Queenie was long-boned, elegant, angular and shiny black. She ran some Byzantine fraud network on the streets, but in jail her general inclination to mayhem had been given free rein.

We got along fine. Certain mutual interests fermented away on the deep shelves of the law library: a hundred feet of tubing, brass gang-valve connectors, half a dozen big jars holding our fruit sugar solution, all hidden behind the yeasty words of federal judges.

We originally said the supplies were for a fish tank. Took us a week to get it set up. Full ferment three days later. The fish died. Too bad.

It needed daily care. Additions. Subtractions. It was magic. Science. Religion. A solution. Freedom of a sort.

We poured the sugar into the warming pan, when it melted we added the juice from the peaches, after a moment set it aside to cool back to body temperature. The yeast in the first jar would die if it got too hot.

Queenie set up the drinks, a couple peach slices in

each of our glasses, a neat tumbler from the final jar poured over them.

"To crime."

"The last frontier."

As we tasted I noticed Queenie side-glancing at me, tried to judge her mood. Nothing was simple with those two.

At last Queenie spoke, ominous undertones, "Your great pal Norah snitched one of my home girls off, got Birdeye locked in the nut ward." She hummed to herself, not looking at me.

I didn't bother to tell her that Norah wasn't a pal. She knew that. Thea picked it up, "China won't leave her cell, she so upset." Thea didn't hum. "They do things to black people back there, Morgan. Surgical. Birdeye might not even survive. Hell, look at Lily."

"And Lily ain't hardly black."

Queenie chuckled evilly, poor Lily's failures were a constant source of amusement. "Birdeye's original beef is just grand theft auto. The girl never can resist a red sports car. She's a mech-anic, no kind of real crim-nal. Now look, Morgan, she could die back there." Queenie gave me the full voltage, eyeball to eyeball. "Talk about justice. Birdeye need to be got outta there. Now."

One two left right pow kapow kapow. This sort of thing might become habitual.

I wasn't comfortable playing these legal games. I didn't have the skill to take it to the courts anyway: citing cases, precedents, esoteric references. That's a job for a rich, well-connected professional. The habeas corpus remedy is a little joke the courts cooked up to keep convicts occupied, let the fusty old judges earn a pension. The little car thief would be dead and stinking before anything got done that way.

Lily's Thorazine-twisted head was already on my conscience, I didn't need a collection of failures, but I thought I might be able to push Birdeye's case as a violation of due process, the fourteenth amendment, that one's not gone yet, even convicts get that one. Modified of course. We get all kinds of rights, at least on paper. If the case was very solid, impressive, I might be able to convince the administration to spring her, then I wouldn't have to try to take it further.

There really wasn't any "further" to take it, I had to win it locally.

I had no idea how I was going to do that.

• THREE •

"Listen, Morgan, this brief is a landmark case." Alexander pushed his hands through his fashionably long hair, looked for a clean place to sit. "This could help you."

"How?" The man kept interrupting my important thoughts. I poked a rude finger at the brief. "It's not retroactive, now is it? No. So it can't apply to me. The courts will consider it at new sentencings, until they find a way around it. So what is it? You need to be told your father is slick?"

Alexander was the only child of a highly respected lawyer. Class. Money. Constitutional law. Their house had an overpriced triple lock on the front door, perhaps a few originals on the walls, statuettes placed on hardwood reproductions, a tidy sum hidden in one of them, under the stairs. Somewhere not very difficult.

I'm always dubious about the quality of goods in lawyers' houses, they seem to have no conception of beauty or even real market value. Tacky shit some of them have. I've broken into enough of their houses to know.

Alexander had just passed the bar exams. He never told me why he'd signed up to work at the prison as a teacher; I never asked, figuring it was just one possible result of a liberal education. I wanted nothing to do with some fancy lawyer posing as a teacher, cruising into a women's prison on a romantic lark, tight little body decorated by designer jeans, linen shirts, expensive shades.

Months of disdain seemed to have done nothing to discourage him. I tried to keep every conversation to the minimum. Answered no questions about my crimes. Past. Present. Or future. Was careful not to seem interested in his background, so he told it to me all the more willingly. I filed it away.

He brought me peace offerings: The latest was his father's brief on the technical loopholes in the laws regarding residential burglaries. A gift that would have been a great help to me personally a few years earlier, it was now useless except as an indication of the frivolous way the law was interpreted at different periods of time. Grunting, I pushed it to one side.

He leaned forward, put his palms flat on my desk, arms stiff. Looking important. He wasn't used to women ignoring him.

"Hey." He felt a lump under the mess of papers, pulled out a good length of half-inch rubber tubing. Curious, he held it up.

I plucked it from his grasp. "Our douche-bag hose."

He set his jaw and left.

That little piece of tubing could have busted our whole damn still. Worse, buried in the clutter there were dozens of little fittings, packets of sugar—abominations in the sight of the law.

I was elbow deep creating chaos out of disorder when Alexander came back. More of his father's work. This time it was on constitutional law. Due process. I stopped shuffling things. I don't believe in coincidence, but Providence should never be ignored.

The brief was concise, to the point, perfect. "Very nice."

His gap-tooth smile was bright as all outdoors.

We spent every spare hour for the next week designing Birdeye an airtight case based on the lack of due process, and reassuring China that progress was being made.

The administration thought it was all my work, so after letting Birdeye out of the nut ward, they held a conference about the difficulties I might make in the law library. They made plans to shift me to another area; then, as these things happen, I got lost in the shuffle of daily prison business.

■　　　■　　　■

The day they let Birdeye back into general population I was searching for one tiny but desperately important citation. Pulling my hair in frustration, swearing like a trucker.

Alexander came sparkling, dancing, smiling into the room. The man had style. Timing. An advertisement from *Gentleman's Quarterly*. I didn't subscribe.

He didn't say a word as I twisted my hair back on top of my head, straightened my mind out, came back to the immediate. I appreciated his silence, if not his wardrobe. He'd been more help with Birdeye than I admitted, it seemed to make his company more bearable. Or maybe he was already looking good to me.

I reached into the bottom drawer of my desk, pulled out two glasses. Poured two stiff ones.

We clicked glasses, "To our first success."

He tasted. He took another sip. Raised an eyebrow at me. I was demure.

"Delicious."

I liked him better all the time.

Birdeye lounged in the doorway, small, dark, bright-eyed, tentative as if poised for flight. She came to get a look at the white broad who'd got her out of the nut ward. She wasn't sure what she'd say, resentful of the obligation. But grateful. "Don't get me wrong now, girl. It's real good to be out of that place. Hey, regular prison lookin' good just now."

She came deeper into the room, looking hard at Alexander. "I still keep an eye out in case some police come up on me with a needle."

I knocked my glass back, motioned to an awkward Alexander to do the same. He downed it in one; while his eyes may have watered, he didn't flinch. "Okay, Morgan."

If he was going to do this kind of thing often he'd need to carry mouthwash with him, to get past the security guards. He said they always wanted to know if he'd gotten any pussy.

He nodded formally to Birdeye on his way out; I didn't

think he liked her tropical dyke look.

She asked, "Who's the pretty little dude?"

Birdeye believed that all educated white people were untrustworthy. I felt like telling her that I wasn't educated, just white, so while there were different rules for me, I still found it easier to deal with people as honestly as possible. Which made me trustworthy. Up to a point.

I skipped all that, answered her question, "He's the English teacher. He's dumb, but he's all right." He certainly seemed harmless enough. I wondered how he was managing with the first serious effects of the hooch. "He's all right."

Pretty little dude. I remarked once about the space between his teeth, asked if he could spit through it. He didn't answer with words, flicked his tongue along his upper lip, smiling at me. Before long I expected to have his fucking house key.

I knocked a cigarette out of the pack, enjoyed the motion, the ritual; with my friendly tobacco demons working again I relaxed under Birdeye's unashamed scrutiny. "Listen, Birdeye, I'm just glad to get you out of there. We almost never win these things, you know." Pompous. "The law's just a tool of the class system, you know."

"Uh. Yeah. Well, thanks. I gotta go." Birdeye had no use for rhetoric.

"No trouble. A pleasure." My mind was already moving forward and backward, chasing the problem down again, trying to find reusable parts. The assault on the system is essentially a process of recycling, that's why it's so unsuccessful.

Birdeye hesitated, half rising out of her chair. "There's one thing I can do for you." She recognized a debt to be repaid. I liked that.

After Birdeye washed the glass Alexander used, we killed what was left in the juice jar. Birdeye explained some of the finer points of brewing.

Scrupulous cleanliness. Boil the jars. Chop the fruit up fine. If bread dough is used for the yeast, that's got to be allowed to ferment first with just a little sugar and juice separately from the main brew. Use a strainer for it, nylon stocking, whatever.

She warmed to her subject. "Regular yeast has to be started separately too, it got a short, explosive life span, die right off if it gets too hot, too cold, there's not enough sugar. Like a baby."

"What about adding soda in an emergency?"

She was horrified. A real professional. "Oh hell no. Keep some sugar syrup warming on the side, ready to add in emergencies."

"Got that already."

She didn't look impressed. "You do it right, you won't have emergencies."

I thought our setup was elaborate before, but I hadn't known shit from elaborate until I saw what Birdeye could do.

• FOUR •

China bent forward, brushing her long black hair. "No tellin' what coulda happened to you back there in Rack, Birdeye, just being in regular prison is enough to make anyone crazy."

Birdeye admired China's smooth back. "You know they been on my case all day? Tellin' me to leave you, find me a black girl. Bitches never let a niggah 'lone." She grinned in a superior way. "Somebody got to watch over you. Figure it might as well be me—you got some of the damnedest ideas."

China straightened up, flipping her mane back over her shoulders, putting her bracelets back on. "Hey, they just be jealous because I never sold this sweet ass of mine—I'm an artist. Didn't have to whore. I worked on important people. Class people. Senators. Judges."

"Nah, you can't tell me that Meskin judges got tattoos?"

"Sure, Birdeye."

"Well, what you doin' in jail now?"

China didn't understand why Birdeye challenged her on every little thing. "They can't get me out no American jail."

China used to have a part-ownership in a tattoo studio in Mexico City, then she hooked up with a gorgeous bronze-skinned North American businessman, moved to the states, prepared for a life of luxury. But the unfortunate Roland Lee was into the business of crime rather than the business of business. It was not kind to him.

The money was good, but never enough—not for her, not for him. Their world was made up of real estate rip-offs, mystery drug scams, bank account bingo. Whenever she complained that it wasn't much of a marriage, he knocked her around. He'd say, "After all I did for you." She answered back in her sharp musical voice, he'd hit her again.

"Only smart thing your husband did was to make you stop tattooin'."

"Bullshit. That was just another thing about the man always did bother me. Think he better than me."

"With you it's always some hassle. You just too stubborn, girl. No wonder these bitches go on."

"They should mind they own damn business."

"Think about yourself, girl. Put some effort into it." Birdeye's small face squeezed tight around her words, "And stop tellin' me lies."

"Lies? Ain't no lies between us, Birdeye!" China leaned to look at herself in the mirror. "Got my own livin' to do, that's all. Hey now, we gone need money on the outside."

"Not like that. I don't want my old lady touchin' people like that. In all that blood. It's disgusting." Birdeye pushed by China, out the cell, didn't look back.

Everyone knew China hadn't killed Roland. The board gave her the shortest time possible, which was still life. A seven-year minimum. For conspiring to kill her husband. Not even for doing it. As if wishing the bastard dead were a punishable offense.

Yet Birdeye insisted that it could have been possible for China to have done it, she'd run it down, how easy it could have been for China to slip away from the bar crowd, blow his brains out.

China claimed the right of lovers to believe in each other, said Birdeye was too paranoid.

Birdeye held her counsel. She was a black girl in jail, and the slaves have yet to be emancipated no matter what they say.

They had the same discussion once a day. As if they would never be quit of it.

China told me, her eyes wide, her voice seductive, how sweet Roland used to be with Varney, the red-headed white bitch with the hungry mouth who worked in his real estate office. "She always be doing little secret things, lean in close to him, talk soft, shooting her eyes at me, putting her hand on his leg. Or the back of his neck. And he smiiiile like a pig in shit."

She shrugged. "Roland kept tellin' me that Varney was the office manager, that we need an Anglo woman to front for us so it looked legit. He say how I could never do that. I was good for the grubby illegal side of things. Supposed to be more money there, but I never got to see it."

She seemed to wait for me to respond. I didn't know how to tell her that I had no intention of helping her look for it.

■　　　■　　　■

"Yo, Morgan!" Alexander poked his head in the law library door, juggling folders and books, panting, eager. "Got a minute saved for me?"

"Oh yaaaah, Alexander," heavy on the exhale, no smoke ring, "come on in."

But Birdeye was in there with me so he dashed off, mumbling some excuse. The fool kept to his own schedule for our encounters, it didn't seem to include company. He and Birdeye were relentless in their hostility. He said she seemed to be a thoroughly unpleasant woman—ugly mannish ways; she muttered dark predictions about terrible things happening to white boys with nothing in their pants but concern. I enjoyed it.

After she'd gone off to the laundry with a couple jars of hooch hidden under a pile of filthy towels, Alexander came back. "What is she, anyway?" Whining. "Is she black or Chinese or Jamaican or what?" He thought he was clever. "You know what the trouble with Birdeye is? She just never was a little girl."

"Try to treat her like a visiting dignitary from a distant galaxy."

"Seemed to touch a nerve there, didn't I?"

"When you don't know shit about something, better keep it to yourself. Things are tough enough without your crap." I didn't like the smug look he'd put on his face that day. "Listen, Alexander, fucking is nice, especially with girls. Drugs are nice. Booze is nice. But nice isn't the point—these things are worth a lot more in here. Survival is measured in commodities, or haven't you noticed?"

A high color touched his handsome upper-class cheeks, he accused me of being drunk. I wanted him to just get the hell out of my life. He said alcohol was dangerous. I knew this game. I took a Sherman cigarette from his pack. "Drunk is one way to do time, Alexander. So is fucking your brains out. There's lots of ways—I got time enough to try them all."

I walked away from him shooting a couple smoke rings dead at his face. "If you're only going to do it once, there's no point in leaving anything out, hey?"

He walked through the smoke, scowling. "I worry about you getting busted for drunk and disorderly. Well, drunk."

I toked up the cigarette until the tip glowed.

"The disorderly is a way of life for you, Morgan. Except for your mind. That has a peculiarly chilling order."

One more step, I'd put it out in his eye.

He stood still then, striking a pose, complaining, "I can't understand why you jeopardize everything for a quick thrill."

"Jeopardize everything? What everything? Listen, you silly prick, the law library's a sham. Freedom through booze, sex or drugs is a lot more likely than through the courts."

Time the man learned that everything didn't always drop off into his hands like ripe fruit. Fresh peaches, but not for you.

He opened his mouth, shut it, turned and stalked from the room. He did it very well.

■   ■   ■

"Man, Birdeye, will you lighten up? Roland wasn't killed at my house. Happened at the real estate office. In the back room on the big leather couch. Another thing Varney nagged him into buying. Wasn't even paid for."

Professional, China moved Birdeye's shoulder a quarter turn to the left, corrected some lines on her sketch of a woman with wings. "He was screwin' her on it. The woman has the morals of a cat. Roland loved the luxury feel of leather, you know, skin. I wasn't anywhere around there when he got dusted."

Birdeye wiggled to see the drawing while China, indulgent, scowled at her. "I had more important things to attend to."

"What? You steppin' out on him?"

"Business. Business. Never no time for steppin' out, girl. There were bank accounts to move around, you know. I wasn't into no petty-ass bullshit. It was real complex. I wasn't no way involved in no murder. You got to believe that."

A silence. Birdeye restrained herself from pointing out that China had hired someone to murder her husband.

China knew better than to try to explain to Birdeye why people would kill people. "You know, something never did feel right about what happened that night. Like Varney, looking shocked and horrified, as if she was the grieving widow." China put her pencil down. "I was the widow. Just because I didn't grieve much—"

"She seem to have played it better than you."

"No shit. The po-lice zeroed in on me so direct I never had no chance to play it no way." China reached for the eraser. "Truth. You know I didn't do it, Birdeye."

Birdeye speculated into the middle distance, "I wouldn't think so. But it's hard to know."

"I still can't figure it out, it isn't as if anyone but you thinks I blew Roland's head off. Everyone in the bar said I'd been drunk as hell that night, all my girlfriends swore I was never out of their sight, we even went to the bathroom together, man."

Birdeye traced designs on China's leg with her index finger, it was difficult enough to be in love without all this other too.

"I don't know how the police found out about Tony the Loser," China giggled, a champagne sound. "I should have known better with a name like that, huh?"

She kissed the top of Birdeye's head. "I set myself up, I guess—just so busy attending to serious money that I didn't pay much attention to the creep I hired—Tony took my three hundred dollars, went off to Reno, lost it all, then got him own self busted; the man try to jimmy a slot machine in a gas station bathroom, was still in a Reno jail when Roland got blown away. Seem to me that that should have cleared me, but for some reason I ended up taking the fall."

Conciliatory, Birdeye murmured, "Not right, that." Short breath. "Why'd you hire someone to kill Roland anyway?"

China added some light shading to the feathers in the drawing, then held it up for Birdeye to see. In a flat emotionless voice she answered simply, "He cut me out."

Simple answers to simple questions. China's public defender told her to plead to the solicitation rather than risk a trial where they'd blow her alibi away, get her for the actual murder. After all, he said, the people willing to testify for her were a bunch of wetbacks and bar whores anyway.

She had been terrified. Yet there were so many other people who wanted Roland dead, seemed someone should have been able to take the weight off her; only a few people knew he was collecting big that evening, it must have been one of them. Or maybe, she once thought, it was a complete stranger. Someone looking for a place to rent just walked in the back room, saw him counting all that money. Shot him, put it in a sack. Left. Clean. A stranger.

She got some slight comfort from that the first few times she'd thought it.

Birdeye gave her a quick kiss, then resumed her study of the drawing.

China ran her palm over Birdeye's cheekbone. "I got to

find out what happened to the money, find whoever has it. It's mine by rights, I earned it. Shit. I bet they haven't dared spend it, worried the police know about it."

Birdeye was only half listening, wondering if she looked that way to China: proud, beautiful, with real big wings.

There was always something crawling at the edge of vision, a ripple of memory, as if someone walked along the perimeter peering in at us, grinning, leaving footprints that burn the ground. Labyrinths, wheels inside wheels. Wax-spiraled floors reflecting off seaweed walls, mermaid-salty voices crooning until you think it wouldn't be so bad to drown. To drown.

• FIVE •

Vertigo. Odd swampy memories mock the uncertain footsteps of new arrivals. You know who's been in for awhile by the ease and security of their tread.

Nothing is provided, yet everything can be found. It's not malicious. Got to be quick. Lamp for your cell, steal it. Fresh air? Rent the window crank from the mean woman down the hall. Sheets? Stay on the good side of the hall's laundry connection. A jar of coffee or a pack of cigarettes open on the mirror ledge? Kiss it good-bye. Still, a home can be made anywhere in spite of dreams of open windows, your own front door. You just have to know the rules.

I first noticed Rosalie the morning she'd diddled the lock on her door, padding it with torn matchbook covers, chewing gum, a paste made from spit and white bread. It stuck closed.

Angry, the guard keyed it open, picked out the crap Rosalie stuffed in there. "You're responsible for your cell, got that, woman? That means the fixtures in it, the condition of your lock and door, you hear? Now I expect this bullshit is over?" His voice rose at the end of every sentence, he fixed her with the standard issue glare. She looked at the floor in embarrassed silence.

He puffed himself up. "What if there been an emergency?"

She stood there with her mouth half open.

"Ooh. Lookit the big white girl blush. Wouldn't think she do like that."

"Every emergency I know of, it be that us get locked in."

The guard looked at the little crowd. "Get a move on, hey." Suspicious bastard.

"What you mean, we responsible for the lock? Well,

what if I takes it upon myself to just leave it permanently unlocked?"

"Okay, ladies, that's enough. Move along. It's time to get your asses to work."

Rosalie didn't look at the crowd, just backed into her cell, closed the door.

Rosalie was a big woman, graceful the way solid heavy women can be. After she graduated from high school she went to work in a bank, developed a beginner's flair for crime, a small desire for pretty things. Diligent, she learned how deposits were handled between branches of the same bank, different banks, what times of the day/week/month various transactions got accomplished, who needs to authorize disbursements of how much, what information was basic for withdrawing funds from any bank, how to dress, speak, move. She was studying finance, she told me, not crime.

She thought about international finance or perhaps stock market schemes: so much to learn, so much money to earn. Thought she was clever setting up a couple dummy accounts for herself with random numbers.

Got herself a modern flat with wall-to-wall; her towels and English soap matched the bath tiles; she put shell-pink satin sheets on the big brass bed; on top of her bleached oak dresser there was a Baccarat crystal bottle filled with the most expensive perfume in the world.

She cultivated the saleswomen in the fur department of a large department store, chatting about dividends from the family's stocks. She was going to buy her mother a fur coat when she got her check, she said. She had her eye on a long silver fox coat, then she thought perhaps she deserved sable after all. A girl's first fur coat is an important decision, she gave it a lot of thought. She could afford anything, after all it wasn't her money.

The latest arrival was a sleek red honey mink, lush to the floor, it went on her shoulders as if it were designed with her in mind. Another mirrored twirl.

It was the perfect time: after five o'clock on the Friday

of a three-day weekend, banks closed until Tuesday. Rosalie thought that she'd worked it to a fine point. Smug. A pro always watches the details.

"Oh yes, does this one have a matching hat?"

She grabbed a bottle of fine champagne out of a bin in the liquor department, handed over the plastic without a thought.

They popped her behind the bogus credit card.

She never adjusted to her mistakes.

■   ■   ■

The visiting room smelled of burnt hair, stale cigarettes, day-old onions, industrial disinfectant. The packaged food dispensers along the wall didn't work. A screaming tension remained unvoiced by mutual consent. Smile, suck in your stomach, smile. There were no easy visits.

I was trying to entertain a well-meaning fellow from the ACLU over coffee and Camels when I saw Rosalie step into the room and kiss her mother. A tall brassy woman, Rosalie's mother always looked sad when she came to visit. Clutching some snapshots, a candy bar, two cream sodas. Holding the threads of dignity in these offerings, a barrier against the hostility, the fear.

Rosalie seemed to think she could be convicted but still not be a convict. She'd got herself a cushy, clean secretary job up front in the administration building, right in the nerve center of the whole place, access to records, a little power. Still didn't know how to do time.

At least she no longer greeted her mother with complicated schemes for escape; they still fenced with each other about their lives, evading the solid things which blocked them. They promised to write more, but they confronted paper with the same trepidation as they faced each other with, minus the immediacy. It should have been easier.

Rosalie shifted her weight, whining. "I worry about you,

Mamma. About me. I'm getting fat. I got wrinkles flabby thighs my breasts are sagging my hair's falling out . . ."

The effects of prison gravity.

"Your uncle been home all this week, just watches the tube, complains. Says your sister's turning into a slut. He says to tell you it's a thankless task, this living, that's why he didn't come this time."

They exchanged a secret grin, began to relax. "Be glad for small favors."

"Who is that odd pale woman—the one who brought the guard coffee and sandwiches?"

"They call her Narcisse the Silent. She's spooky."

I was sensitive about how people talked about my cell-mate.

"Deaf and dumb," Rosalie shivered. "You never know what she's thinking. Or even if she's thinking. Never know, it might rub off?"

"Like color—oh I do hope you're being careful, dear."

Rosalie grabbed her mother's hand, rubbed her knuckles. "Don't worry, Mamma, I don't go near them."

I didn't think I liked Rosalie very much.

Rosalie went back to the unit, locked in her cell, painted her toenails "Fascination Peach" drying them by walking one two three pivot on the left foot one two three pivot on the right at the cot one two three pivot at the door. She kept it slow. It was something to do.

Birdeye usually decided to run the floor polisher after a fight with China; she flew from one side of the hall to the other, grinning and hanging onto the bucking handles, spiraling galaxies in the thick floor wax.

A barometer of sorts.

In her frenzy Birdeye slammed into Rosalie's door, already closed.

Sharp, mischief-filled eyes. "Hey wow. Hey. I'll tell the pig to pop it back open, I'm really sorry, Rosalie."

Rosalie hollered to forget it, she wanted to be safe with her own miserable thoughts, locked in all alone. Safe. Unless there was a fire. Then she'd fry.

Birdeye came back dragging a tamed floor polisher, the cell opened like sesame.

"So. How's it goin'?"

Rosalie shrugged, uncomfortable. She'd just told her mother she avoided these people. She was caught at a disadvantage. Sighing, Rosalie invited Birdeye in.

Birdeye examined her cell. "Nice. Lucky not to have anyone sharin' your house. This prison so small—everybody in everybody else's shit—don't nobody have a life of their own. You know what I mean? You got to divide it up: This much for the bitches on the block, that for your old lady, something other for your family—a whole other part for your enemies. Got to feed them all."

Rosalie wasn't sure.

"Trouble with women is they're women. You know. But I don't like men. Never did. There just aren't enough places on 'em, you know?"

Rosalie didn't know.

"Men been trying to do me all my life, sneak it up on me, saying you black or what? What *is* you anyway, honey? Oooh you sure is pretty. C'mon home with me, we'll make beautiful babies. What are you sweet thing sweet thing."

Rosalie sort of nodded but she had no idea.

"Hey listen, then I started to develop breasts, you know, the guys'd come up to me, do this cat in cream routine. I didn't know too much but I knew I didn't want that." She moved her hands around her body. "I used to wrap a Ace bandage around me so they wouldn't show.

"Then I realized that I liked girls. Hey!" she grinned, stretching. "That was the end of one set of problems and the beginning of another."

Stiff, uncertain, "Sounds like you got some personal problems."

"Yeah. I got personal problems. Everybody got personal problems. Everybody's got some opinion about it too. But try to get a straight story out of anyone, see where it gets you."

Birdeye began to talk to the corners of the cell then,

pacing, "China got one of those minds. One of those minds, she's a real artist. She never need to work at it, it just come to her."

Rosalie wondered where this was going. Her headache was starting to make blue halos around things, as if she'd been sniffing lighter fluid.

"Hey." Birdeye demanded her attention. "Took me all Sunday to put those shelves up for her in there, had to be just so." Birdeye shook her head. "Now she says I'm supposed to put the shelves up along the other wall, where the sun won't dry out her paints. I don't know."

"Hey mija! There you are!" China appeared in Rosalie's cell waving an odd gadget about the size of her hand, the electrical cord swinging. "Hello, Rosie. 'Scuse me for interrupting." Close look at Birdeye. "Said, 'Sorry for interrupting.' Aren't you gonna say nothin'?"

"Right." Serious. "What the hell is that thing?"

"I bought it from Narcisse." China twirled around the cell in ecstasy. "Even got me some proper ink!"

She stopped, looked at their blank faces. "Don't you guys understand?" No reaction. "Tattoos? Entiendes?" She figured that Birdeye would get excited by the mechanics of the thing at least. "See? The motor drives the needle up and down a million times a second. I can do fine work now."

"That's great. Just great." Birdeye blew her breath out in a rush. "What you want to go be—touching—all that blood. You got to quit that jailhouse thinking. You an artist."

"Aw, don't give me that shit. Listen, if people want to mark theyselves in here at least they can bid for the best. That's me, Birdeye. I'm the best."

"The best? Tattoos? Big fucking deal. You listen to me, I don't like no woman of mine hammerin' on people."

Rosalie tried to get them both to leave.

China gave her a venomous look. Nobody pushed her around. "Hey, Rosalie, I heard some flashy little whorina saying as how she thought she could do your job better than you, she being a professional and all."

Birdeye edged toward the door. "Not enough air in here. How they expect a nigger to breathe?"

China turned on her. "What's the matter, Birdeye?"

"You and this fucking tattoo bullshit!" Birdeye slapped the palm of her hand flat to China's shoulder, shoving her against the wall.

Rosalie fluttered around trying to stay out of the way, cracked her coffee cup on the corner of a shelf; Birdeye backed into it, a solid connection, there was blood and coffee all over Rosalie's black velvet rug with the picture of a tiger.

"Oooh." China checked to see that the damage wasn't fatal, did a quick fade, leaving Birdeye, who couldn't think what to do, and Rosalie, who lived there, to deal with the mess.

Rosalie moaned as she attempted to sop up the blood.

Birdeye remarked, unconcerned, "The administration will ban all china on the blocks now. You know they banned Tampax once, claiming someone suicided herself by choking on one."

• SIX •

Officer Johnson, still wearing her uniform a size too small, rubber-soled it down the hall, nosed into Rosalie's cell. She turned the color and texture of curdled milk, backed away just far enough to miss adding to the mess inside the cell.

"Wuh. Lookit that. Dinner and all kinds of awful stuff."

"Bitch goes and pukes all over our floor and then, well you know sheee ain't gone clean it up—not herrrrrr. Oh no. That's dead."

"We gotta live with this shit. My mamma didn't raise me to live like they do around here."

Johnson tried to make us go lock in, she slopped on her new shoes, threatened everybody with disciplinary action: disrespect for an officer, refusing a direct order, *insubordination*. "You'll all be locked in your cells forever," she pushed a pudgy hand up against her running nose, "and I'll be glad!"

Rosalie's boss, the watch commander, strolled in. Hand-tooled cowboy boots. Nice, ah, muscle tone. Well-tailored uniform like a highway patrolman's. He looked at the mess, the pale policewoman, the glinty-eyed convicts, did not crack a smile when a voice sneered out, "See? I told you! Just you wait 'til your father gets home."

"She started it, Dad, honest."

Rosalie groaned.

He remained impassive. Arms folded. Aloof. The only problem he saw was the guard's inability to control her stomach or her prisoners. He'd give Rosalie a lecture about the company she was keeping, that would end it. Unless of course she was in the habit of cutting up her lovers.

"Okay. Show's over. I want to get you to the med station, Birdeye, you may need a stitch. Officer Johnson, please go call for an escort, wash yourself up. I'll talk to you in Control. The rest of you ladies please lock yourself in, we will be doing count in three minutes." The drawling voice of authority. He barely nodded to Rosalie.

Officer Johnson thought that the Cowboy and Rosalie were involved in something. Sordid. She knew all about that sort of thing. She knew how important these reports were, how precious all the details. A conspiracy gone wrong. A plot to incite to riot. Or mayhem. Or murder. Suicide?

No one was let back out for showers.

"Gone be some funky smelling whores walking the circle tomorrow. I ain't gone to work with 'em. No way."

■   ■   ■

Counselor Claudia O'Neill was a big cheerful country girl grown up right there in the valley, taking a job at the prison came as natural to her as clerking at the corner store. Never much bothered by the way one decision led to another and another, the inevitability of the way things happened, she'd just find herself in a situation, do the simplest thing.

Early the next morning Claudia held Johnson's report from the night before in her left hand, the disciplinary ticket for Rosalie in the other, wondering half-aloud why some people want to work in corrections, they were so well suited to menial jobs. Unfortunately the disciplinary hearing officers, nuts all of them, were not likely to recognize the report as ravings of a lunatic. Or perhaps they would. It made no difference.

Claudia liked Rosalie. Both big women. Usually their conversation centered around weight. Hips. Thighs. Weight. Sometimes sex. They made it out to be less important than it was.

She unlocked Rosalie's cell, stepped into the doorway. "What's shakin', Rosie?"

Rosalie's hands. Her eyes shot nervous glances at the

ticket. She tried to be clever, "I heard your old man went and got religion. No fornication without procreation, ain't that a bitch?" Her laugh didn't quite work.

Claudia was newly married, home life wasn't all that great since the husband had gotten God. Lucky she was strong minded, she said, could do what needed to be done. She worked overtime a lot now, stopped at the corner bar on her way home, drank a beer or two with the big smiling man working there; Claudia never realized how susceptible she was to the subtle charms of a happily muscled male. He was from some tropical island. She used him to fill those empty dream spaces in her life, she didn't suppose he'd mind.

"I surely don't like this God thing, Rosalie. Not at all. If my husband and God have such a close relationship they probably talk about me when I'm out of the room." She pouted, "Don't do shit for my sex life."

Rosalie didn't care.

"I mean, what sex? Rosalie. Listen. Don't ever get married. Not even to a guy that's taller 'n you."

"What's that you got in your hand, Claudia?"

Attempted murder, perhaps suicide, refusal to disperse or cooperate, insubordination. *Heads will roll.* If they don't get you coming in, they'll trip you on the way out.

Rosalie cajoled, "Don't give that ticket to me, Claudia. Johnson is out of her freaking mind. And Birdeye's nuts anyway." Her voice slipped gears, "Nothing happened last night, Claudia, believe me." Her eyes got large, sort of watery.

We loitered in the hall, cradling our morning coffees.

Uncomfortable, Claudia said, "Oh hell. Come up to Control where we can both sit down." And we couldn't hear.

Rosalie's voice came out low, something about caught in a flood of events, insignificant things snagged on underwater trees. I liked the image. Her voice got stronger, "It's so demeaning. Oh, Claudia," a hiccup, "I can't believe you're doing this."

Claudia was firm. "Come up to Control."

"I don't deserve this kind of treatment." Rosalie glared around as if it were our fault.

■   ■   ■

The hearing officer sighed, "A typically annoying affair."

Rosalie had used the word "metaphysical" to clarify her position.

"Well. Officer Johnson is new on the job."

"A difficult situation."

The other one, plaintive, "Well. There was apparently a *lot* of blood."

They told Rosalie to go wait in the hall.

She leaned against one of the glass partitions dividing up the administration building. No solid walls in this area, someone always had to be watching; statistics made it clear that hundreds of crimes happened every moment, the only defense was constant vigilance. A young guard stared at Rosalie from forty feet and two rooms away, waiting for her to do something peculiar.

Rosalie put her mind on hold, worked on her face. She raised her eyebrows, blinked like an animal shaking itself after something nasty touched it, settled her face into near immobility. Not enough to relax the muscles, the features that make a face exist must blur: forehead nose cheeks lips chin, mere knobs of clay on a barren landscape, the eyes become saline lakes, flat, purely reflective surfaces.

The face must work like a wall, stop the stare a quarter inch before it hits the skin. Invisibility is the ultimate goal.

Rosalie stood at the foot of the Formica conference table staring at the crumbs, she felt her stomach lurch, that same twisting falling sensation as in the first court-room.

"Listen to me now, young woman, homosexuality and drugs will ruin your life! The stigma will follow you wherever you go, whatever you do!"

Stigma? She stared into the hole of his greasy mouth, missing the way his eyes floated around her body.

Moist lips, tasting the words, "You were sentenced to our correctional facility because you were a threat to society, but you seemed to be doing well. Adjusting. Until this incident?"

Another one, deliberate. "There was nothing on your record to suggest that you're a practicing homosexual. Are you?"

"Am I what?" Her mind reeled. Practicing? Like rehearsals? As opposed to what? Performing? Her?

Insinuation. "You're a well-educated young woman, why do you hang around with dykes?"

"Because I'm in jail?" She wasn't trying to be flip.

"You don't seem understand the seriousness of the offense, Rosalie. This sort of near-anarchy can not be tolerated. Not in our prison. You will be given a month closed custody, reassigned to the morning shift in the cafeteria. We'll review your status at the end of the month."

She kept her face blank, her head up. Her feet moved one in front of the other taking her back to her cell. "I'm the only one who can keep the fucking watch commander's paperwork in order—ninety-nine point nine percent of these bitches can't even spell their alias. Just goes to show. Try to do a good job. Shows how much they appreciate what I do." Muttering. She didn't look at us.

Prison metaphysics can be a lifetime study. Rosalie would never know what the word meant. She used it because it rolled off her tongue in a rich powerful way.

The whole damn prison would collapse into total absolute chaos if it wasn't for convict labor. If it wasn't for crime there wouldn't be convicts, then these people'd be shit out of a job. But they never think of that. Never yet seen a grateful guard.

• SEVEN •

Birdeye made combinations of ordinary products that could "help you sleep, wake you up, spin you around, girl, even make you forget where you are. Got it all in my pockets. Um-hum, um-hum."

They'd emptied her pockets before they locked her back in Rack again.

She lay like a mummy on the narrow cement ledge, the single blanket folded under her. She stopped trying to tug it up around her shoulders because her legs got cold, then she got tired of curling up like a baby with the cold creeping up her back. So she played dead. Her side throbbed where she'd cut it on the cup.

The squeeze had been on her the last few days, everything seemed to be getting cracks in it, sawdust everywhere she touched. Tiny spiders sucked her dry, left gaps filled with cobwebs and dead bugs. Her mind, that dusty pit, assured her that she wasn't going over the edge, just stirring the ashes around one more time.

She traveled up her spine from the base to the joint of her neck, then through her shoulder muscles, under her arm along the nerve fibers, past old injuries. She surrounded the cut flesh with warmth, touched it with the fourth finger of her opposite hand, hummed an odd satin-ribbon kind of tune, over and over, the notes blending into each other sssss until they bit their own tails, turned into spinning circles, healing.

Pain sounds go on continually in prison, the whole place tight with the agony of wounds unhealed, real and imagined, bleeding, each shrieking in its own key. Always the memories, the sounds of the last woman, the next. In the corners, counting the days, the ways, the women, the pain all the way back to the beginning, small as a sliver of glass in sand. So few people visit the dead.

China had no pity for the dead. "I save what little of it there is for the living." She shrugged, smiling. "Some."

Birdeye never wanted anyone dead. Not really. Well, not for long, it was a fleeting thing with her; now and again she'd figure the world would be better without this one or that one, but she never got worked up about it. Not, certainly, enough to kill someone.

In the normal way it was hard to think of China as a killer, then Birdeye thought maybe it might happen again; killing off her lovers might become a habit?

If China hadn't killed Roland, who had—Roland's own brother? That man still visited China, ran for her, strutted for her. Another one of her adoring fans. Shit. Or what if Tony the Loser wasn't the only one she'd hired?

Birdeye imagined dozens of guys running around trying to dust China's husband, win China as the prize in some bizarre sweepstakes?

Birdeye sat up, wrapped the blanket around her shoulders, pictured herself and China living together in a little wooden house with a cat, a red sports car maybe, a lawn in front she cut every Saturday. Why in hell murder someone anyway? The earth was so big. Just move away.

Birdeye thought she'd never been so lonely, so confused. She let her mind wander over to the corners.

The screamers were there. Liars. Deceivers.

There was no place safe, no safe place.

They came creeping sneaking whispering: Come closer come closer—

Come up come up the steps, fear not the slippery edge, fear not the reddish smell, fear not the dripping knife, come up come up come up the steps.

Blood-burned memories, like old footprints on the steps, scream against the progress even as we move toward the edge; the ancient voices whisper: Come up come up the steps, fear not the slippery edge, fear not the reddish smell, fear not the dripping knife—join us come to us join with us.

All that matters is the edge and the knife.

Come up the steps.

• EIGHT •

The distant crashing of the cell doors woke us every morning around six, we wiggled toes, opened eyes, stretched, padded over to the sink. Splash face. Rinse mouth. Totter out to the laundry room for hot water, add instant coffee. Three sugars. Go back home. Stare in the mirror. Look awful. Light cigarette. Drink coffee. Look better. We depended on certain rituals. A necessary, intricate process.

An hour or two before dawn Rosalie was zapped with a million volts of light. Fried her eyeballs right in the sockets. Cursing like a banshee she leaped from her cot. "What the hell is going on—what is it with you anyway— fucking savage!"

She rummaged for her clothes, throwing things around, trying to stay asleep. "What the fuck time is it anyway? Sweet Jesus."

The guard stepped back a pace, her mouth opening and shutting in silent surprise.

"Stop that! You look like a fish."

Rosalie's neighbor crooned in her liquid gold voice, "Rosie. Rosie. You working in the cafeteria this morning. Now just go on over there, leave us sleep."

Rosalie was stunned. "Fuck all." She pulled on a sweatshirt. "I hope that the whole administration collapses." Two pairs of socks. "Hey, it's not my job to keep this shithole running. I don't care if the whole thing falls over on its side like a dead horse." Pulled on sweat pants. Peacoat. "If we ever refused to work the police just push us into the cells, set the damn blocks on fire. Smoke us to death. No question." Smashed a watch cap on her head.

"Hush now, Rosie, it's not that bad."

"Fuck you it's not."

No one normal wants the first goddamn shift.

Crunching across the dead grass toward the cafeteria she curled her mind up as tight as her fists frozen deep in her pockets. The guard watched her for any sign that she might rush off toward the fence, fling herself on the razor wire. It was the furthest thing from her mind.

They pushed through a closet-sized security room between bulging file cabinets.

Queenie, the lieutenant's secretary, elegant even at dark-thirty in the morning, looked at Rosalie with contempt. "Some stupid shit you got yourself into this time."

Rosalie sighed. She hadn't even gotten a cup of coffee.

Pots. Pans. Filth. Rosalie was covered with sweat, cheap detergent, foul water, her thoughts were slippery beyond language, unspeakable. Infernal machines somewhere in the cavernous blue distance whined and wailed, she faced a double washbasin the size of a bathtub, towering beyond her reach were hundreds of grimy forty-gallon cook pots, behind her a machine as big as a dumpster sprayed hot water, raving. The smallest particle of grease or gum made the steam machines scream; gears grinding, life as she knew it ceased. The excitement was nonstop.

"God, this is the pits." Rosalie shrugged to herself in horror, she knew better than to try to talk to these people.

Thea was, unfortunately for Rosalie, bossing the sinks that day. Unsympathetic and mischievous, she turned a blank stare on Rosalie as if surprised that she could talk.

Rosalie knew of Thea and Queenie from the mug shots she'd filed for the watch commander in another life, a softer life, a clean easy life. She already thought of it with nostalgia. She was unable to recall what Thea was in for. Dope? Murder? Mayhem? No matter how bad things were they could always get worse.

Thea remarked, smooth as Jack Daniels, "It not so bad. We don't get bothered much, have nearly all day free, you know—" She pointed with her chin in a rude fashion up toward the administration building. "We don't have to do no ass kissin', we don't have to work near no police. Seems ideal."

"Aw." Rosalie wanted to crawl under the sink and hide.

Queenie leaned on the steam machine, casual. Deadly. "We hear you and Birdeye was rippin' it up Sunday—Birdeye got thrown in Rack now?" It was a rhetorical question. Rosalie felt sweat trickling down her sleeves. "And you got sent over to us degenerates to do some serious thinking?" Queenie leered.

Rosalie never knew who was dangerous. Only time would clear that up. In time everything got cleared up, but she didn't know how much time she herself personally had left. She didn't want to have that much time here at the mercy of these two ferocious women, God only knowing what sort of people they were, in prison she could meet just about any kind, a girl can't be too careful, crazy things happen inside that an ordinary criminal never imagined.

She grabbed another greasy pot and splashed cold cruddy water over herself. Gasping, she snarled, "Fuck all. My mamma didn't raise me to be no pot scrubber."

"That's too bad. But I bet she didn't raise you to be no criminal either, girl."

Outclassed. Tips of her fingers shriveled, face red from the slop and steam, blowing like an old draft horse, Rosalie prayed for a break.

After an appropriate time Queenie suggested that they all step outside on the loading dock, take care of some business, smoke a cigarette. Perhaps Rosalie could give her fellow slaves a menthol cigarette?

Slaves? "Ah. I don't seem to have any cigarettes." Doom.

"Perhaps she be willing to loan you a couple." Thea shot her eyes at a lithe muscular blonde woman wearing starched Levi's, a blood-stained apron, a death's head T-shirt rolled up above her biceps.

Rosalie suffered from a definite lack of proper social training, she never planned on hanging out in this society, another one of her mistakes, she should have begun educating herself as soon as she'd thought to get into a life of crime. She didn't have time to learn proper manners now.

The blood-covered madwoman appeared to be grinding weird animal parts into sludge. Rosalie approached her crablike, sideways, tiptoe.

The butcher stopped her machine, grinned at her. "Be real careful, girl, those two can eat you up for breakfast." She shook three cigarettes from her pack of Kools. "Could be the end of you." She seemed to find something amusing.

Rosalie clutched the cigarettes in damp hands.

The mayhemmers were on the loading dock conferring over a plate of pancakes and eggs. Thea lifted her fork, waved it at Rosalie. "So listen to this now, honey— I'm talking about that little cunt who's doing your job up front now—she only likes them tough white bulldaggers, girl, or men or something. Her first day on campus she went right on up to Deuce and said, like she be *ex*-perienced, 'My nose is wide open.' She lean forward, you know, to show some tit, she say, 'Looks real good, I think I'm going to like it here.'"

Rosalie smiled half-assed in response, not knowing. Not much wanting to know, but wanting to know all the same.

"Deuce gives her that flat-eyed look, tells her how she wouldn't let her suck her asshole clean."

"What?"

"What." Imitation. "What." Huge unstoppable laughter, doubled over, leaning onto Rosalie so she needed to hold them both up.

Grunting, Rosalie remarked that she didn't know that she understood word one. They fell all over themselves laughing again.

"One of these days you guys can explain to me just what is so funny." She ignored the egg yolk dribbling down her leg. "Right now I just want to, ah, enjoy the view."

They were on a loading dock eight feet above the asphalt turnaround; beyond that a barren earth field disappeared in fog long before it got to the fence.

"What'd you say? I mean—you do keep an attitude, don't you, girl?"

"She doesn't want to get down with Deuce after all?"

Rosalie realized she'd have to suck on every word. "What?"

"Don't you know about the butcher? Always looking for fresh meat to carve up."

"Oh." Rosalie wished she could go lock in her cell.

"See," Queenie spoke as if she were speaking to a small child, "that girl up front what's doin' your job now tried to get Deuce, when that didn't work she try to set Deuce up. But Deuce be above all that. That girl wouldn't even be walkin' if she wasn't hidin' out in your old job up front now."

"See? And you're back here with us and Deuce." Thea was gleeful. "What goes around—"

Why her? Why now? Why Birdeye and that awful guard Johnson and these horrible women with their dangerous ideas glittering in their ferocious eyes when all Rosalie ever wanted was money enough for a little house in the suburbs or maybe a condo with a view in town? A safe quick screw now and then.

"Hey!" Thea poked her. "What did Deuce say to you?"

"I didn't listen."

"What? You looked interested enough."

"Your nose wide open, girl."

Rosalie knew now that she would go mad in days rather than months. "I don't know what she said. She seemed to be warning me about you two."

"Ain't that the way it always is." More of that unnerving laughter. "You try do someone a favor, they stab you in the back."

"See if we go pimping for her again."

Thea shook a cigarette out of her own pack, offered it to Rosalie. "Well it's not much of a life, but it'll do."

Rosalie took it, wondering why they sent her to bum cigarettes off that crazy butcher when they had a whole damn pack.

"Got a light, hey?"

She jumped, then fidgeted around a lot to cover up. Deuce, the demon butcher dyke, moved as quiet as a cat. Rosalie patted her pockets in a useless manner. Thea and Queenie had done a quick fade, smirking.

"That's okay. They probably be all wet anyway." Deuce took Rosalie's cigarette, lit her own off it, blew the smoke into the fog. "How long you been in?"

"Five months."

"Only a minute."

"Seems forever." Uncomfortable, Rosalie blundered onward, "What are you in for?" It seemed an innocuous question.

"Life." Deuce kept her face neutral, disconnected. "Murder One. Yes I did it and no I'm not sorry." She turned a pair of eyes as clear and empty as a mountain lake on Rosalie. "Like the guy who dropped the bomb on Nagasaki, thinking he did the right thing—all of a sudden there's all these dead bodies everywhere. He's gonna feel sorry? Sorry?"

Rosalie stood there with her mouth open in a sort of mystical horror.

• NINE •

Early one morning Deuce caught the fat dietitian down on her knees sucking off the maintenance man, as if the cow couldn't do that sort of thing on her own damn time. Deuce figured they'd discipline the woman even if she was one of their own; instead Deuce got stuck overnight back in Rack, the maintenance man came and went with his zipper at half-mast, the dietitian continued to spit in the soup: Daily, weekly, monthly, tax-free money skimmed right off the top. Perhaps she owned stock in the place.

Deuce didn't give up.

Wednesday afternoon Lily was rotating like a small giddy planet in front of the cafeteria. "Them turkeys done drowned, don't you know."

"What's that crazy whore up to now?"

Lily said, "Turkeys don't know enough to get out of the rain. They just stands there and drowns."

"That's right. That's right."

"That fat woman in there buys our dinners. But she don't save the state any money. Oh no." Lily moved on to another part of the crowd. "Now, we don't pay no taxes, do we?"

"What is it?" Hissing.

"So what we care if they rip the taxpayers off behind drowned turkeys?"

Inside we continued to push green things around our plates: a ladle of greenish potatoes, slimy lettuce, green turkey, squares of green jello at the end of the line. It was one of the green meals, vestiges of a harvest we never see. Oh green was my valley and the food therefrom.

"Hey! What is this shit?"

We crowded around the steam table to get a look while the server stood stony-faced, ladle in hand.

Drowned turkey? Tomorrow was Thanksgiving.

Thea and Queenie thought drowned turkeys were the funniest thing since the little burrowing owl bit a chunk out of Old Norah's ear.

"Attention, ladies."

General shuffling. Rising voices.

"Ladies! Ladies!"

The lieutenant screamed over the intercom that the goddamn turkeys had not drowned, they were regular turkeys bought special for Thanksgiving. "If you don't want to eat your dinner that's your decision. But please don't spoil it for those who want to have a nice dinner."

"I ain't gone eat that shit no way—"

"More for me then, you stupid whore. Did you think that could be true? No way. They couldn't do that."

"The hell they couldn't—where you grow up anyway, girl?"

"No, come on, girl, these ain't no drowned turkeys."

"What you know from turkeys anyway—I ain't gone eat it."

"Food here's nothin' to miss anyway. I be damned if I come here for dinner again."

"Good, then I don' hafta see you talkin' with yer mouth full."

China's voice rose above the rest, "What you got to do is go up, give that turkey a real good look, I mean now, look it right in the ol' eye. Or whatever—then you realize what you got to do is—"

"Ladies! This is not a town hall. Sit down and eat your dinners or go back to your units."

"This shit's got to stop." China threw her dinner in the garbage can. "I think we got an attempted murder here. They be tryin' to poison us."

"Now there's some serious talk there—"

"Murder. Hey. There be laws against that!"

"Ladies! It's a frozen count, ladies. Go back to your cottages. Go back to your cottages. It's a frozen count."

China said "Goddamn" to no one in particular. "Came out of my cell for this?"

．   ．   ．

No one was comfortable as the prison prepared for the winter holidays. In the dingy control room Claudia slumped over the gray metal desk she shared with the guards. The watch commander stood looking around the little room, critical. "Somebody is going to have to clean this place soon, at least wash the windows, you can't hardly see to the end of each corridor now, woman."

I happened to be passing by, overheard the Cowboy say, "Does Rosalie have something going with that crazy nigger—was it a lover's quarrel? Does Rosalie carve up her lovers as a general thing?"

He always claimed to know everything. Big stud. Ho.

Claudia sounded cross. "Is that relevant, Cowboy?"

"Listen, woman, I don't care if it is relevant. Is it true?"

High-handed bastard.

She huffed at him, "Don't be silly. Nothing like that goes on with my girls."

"Balls." Cowboy stomped out of Control, nearly tripping over me as I fumbled for nothing on the floor. I wondered if the man was going to let Rosalie get stuck in the cafeteria because he thought she was getting it on with Birdeye. Rather funny in a way.

Claudia growled out to the hall after him, found me. "Hey, Morgan. During count I want you to wash these windows. Looks like a pigsty."

I gave Claudia the slow sideways look, cool as shit. "That's because it is a pigsty." This bright repartee develops through years of practice.

■   ■   ■

At eight o'clock that night when all the women on closed custody locked in, Rosalie had already fallen out on her bunk. She couldn't sleep, wallowing in the day's horrors on the wide screen of her mind, seemed she'd got a bit part in a B movie, part of someone else's diabolical design.

China wandered down the hall, found herself at Rosalie's locked door. Lights out. She pushed her face against the wicket hole, whispered, "Hey, Rosalie, you in there?"

Mumblings and rustlings, the light came on. "I am now. What's up?"

"Aw. I'm sure Birdeye hates me."

"Right. Sure. Look, China, it's nobody's fault. Blame it on the judge that put you here or something. Birdeye just gets all twisted, takes it out on you—" Rosalie felt she'd spend the rest of her time squished up against her cell door, urgent, talking through a very small opening about nothing, mouth to ear.

"Well it doesn't seem right." China switched eyes. "Hey, Rosalie, was that true about the turkeys or what?"

"How should I know? I think Deuce just made it up and let Lily run with it."

"It worked good though, huh?"

Rosalie couldn't see the point. "She was just making unnecessary trouble."

"Aw, Rosalie, you don't understand."

Rosalie hadn't expected anyone to bother with Lily, or the turkeys. Busy as she was with her own change of fortune, it seemed irrelevant. Silly. But when she saw the panic in the dining hall and the gleam of a smile on Deuce's face, she trotted straight back to her cell, got down on her knees to pray that Cowboy would call her back to work up front.

"You're right, China. I don't understand. I don't want to understand. Good-night."

■　　■　　■

I was the next stop on China's trek. She stretched out full length on Narcisse's bunk. "Where's Narcisse?"

"Finishing up at the canteen. Want to stay for a snack?"

"Thanks—I can't. Got to watch my weight. Squish Bird-eye." She waved a negligent hand along her body, I didn't see any extra weight, thought she could eat all she wanted, come on and squish me. Oh yes.

Narcisse came in smiling, nodded to China, handed her a kite from Birdeye. Kissed me on the cheek, whipped out a pint of chocolate chip ice cream. The heavens opened up.

China looked up from the kite. "Birdeye says I shouldn't have anything to do with the people from my past, she says I can't see Leonard any more, that he set me up. Well, shit, Leonard can't have set me up."

Between bites, "Who the hell is Leonard?"

"My husband's brother. Dead husband. Whatever. We still have a lot to do with each other, you know how it is with business." I knew that sly tone; even Narcisse, unhearing, knew it. But China smiled like an angel. "Birdeye can't stand my seeing him. Since Rosalie knows all about banks, I think she be just the person to be our go–between. It will be perfect. Leonard's such a sweetheart, he'll do anything, just give him a pretty girl to work with."

Narcisse's eyebrows rose until they nearly left her face, her fingers flew.

I translated for China: "She says 'You mean your husband's brother is taking care of you in here when you're doing time for trying to have the man offed?' That's weird, China."

China shrugged as if it were of no consequence. "Birdeye's jealous, I guess it be best not to have Leonard visit me. Makes her crazy."

"So tell the man come every other month?"

She waved the cigarette she'd snagged from my pack. "You don't understand. I need him. Money." Palm up. "So I think I'll lend him to Rosalie."

Like I said, I never know what's going on in China's mind. "What if she doesn't want him?" Again, "How come the brother of the guy you tried to kill is so damn concerned about your welfare anyway?"

"He knows I didn't do it." Slow luxurious stretch, rising off the cot like a dancer, clear light shining. "You can bet your snatch that Rosalie will want him."

Something about this made me nervous. I put the ice cream down, followed her into the hall. "He knows you paid someone to do it. Everyone knows that. Now even if that little creep you hired couldn't do it, Roland's brother can't feel kindly toward you. Unless of course, he had it in for his own brother."

"Oh no." Timed right on the beat. "He knows what trouble I get myself into—"

I wondered if her tongue would turn black from lying. It didn't seem so. I whispered, "You covering for him or something?"

China nuzzled my shoulder, whispering back, "He's a very loving man."

"And you?" I liked the feel of her face on my shoulder.

"Ah me." Flirting. Secure. "Love is always second to business." Even brighter. "But then again, everything changes. I don't see what this has to do with anything. Give them both a thrill."

"There's some compelling thing about, about passion—I've never understood it, but then, I'm not much of an expert on love."

"I know." She swayed away from me down the hall.

• TEN •

Thanksgiving morning the police moved in their ritual patterns, counting the bodies. Deuce kept her radar loops working, continual reports on the situation and the surroundings. Survival. Automatic. Test the currents, tensions, interplay. She knew without a clock it was almost time.

She felt Rosalie watching her with an innocent, hungry look.

Deuce was not the least interested in turning anyone out: It became a theater piece, the weight of responsibility, the burden of someone else's sexuality, the whole phony edifice of sociology on her shoulders. Hell, she longed for the time when dykes were in the closet and the sociologists were underemployed.

Rosalie was one of those women who didn't know what she wanted. Should go talk to a sociologist. Deuce wasn't going to explain it to her. Nine minutes to go.

Deuce chopped the slimy turkeys up, flipping the parts expertly onto the exact center of the sheets of wax paper, green side up every time.

Rosalie watched her.

Eight minutes. The guard started his rounds.

Deuce shut down the machine, dropped the turkey packages into the cart, strolled over to the double sinks, weightless, casual, on the balls of her feet, steady. She washed her hands with lots of soap, dried them on Rosalie's towel. Her voice held a thin lilt, "Hey, come on, one of you. Help me move this cart onto the back loading dock?" Ready.

"Well. I like that." Thea glared in surprise as Rosalie stepped away from her sink and fell into step with Deuce. Set.

"Your turn in ten minutes, Thea. Moving quick today."

"Fuck that. Me first."

"All right. Hustle up."

Go. Thea sauntered ahead of them as Rosalie pushed the cart with Deuce. When they turned the corner Rosalie saw Queenie holding up a roll of gaffer's tape and a huge pair of scissors, Thea's shirt was pulled up, muscles and tattoos for days. Rosalie gasped, frantic, she figured she was going to get killed, or raped, she looked around for a guard, not a one.

Deuce pulled out a steak wrapped in butcher paper, slapped it against Thea's naked belly. Queenie taped it in one swift movement. Snip. Less than a minute.

"Hurry up there, dear, or it's drowned turkey tonight."

Rosalie took a step away. "Oh I couldn't."

Queenie stood in her way. "Got some invoices for you." She handed them to Rosalie. "Pass 'em on to Morgan."

"What?" Rosalie sputtered. "Those turkeys didn't drown. I don't want your damn invoices." Wiggling away from Deuce. "This steak is stolen from I don't know where—"

Queenie put her face directly in Rosalie's, purring. "What you know about it?"

"Just that, umm . . . " Rosalie felt Deuce move closer. "Aw, nothing. I just don't think I can do this."

"But you are." Deuce brushed her fingertips across Rosalie's stomach, held the steak in place as she reached around behind to tape the invoice file to her flip side. "Bring it by B-side tonight, you sweet thing, I'll cook it up for us." Deuce's eyes glittered. "The steak. The steak."

She slapped Rosalie on the ass to send her away but Rosalie stopped, turned back, as if to protest again. Deuce took her by the shoulders, pulled her toward herself, put a proper lip lock on her. Might as well give the big girl what she wanted.

Rosalie flattened herself along the length of Deuce's firm body, wrapping herself right around her, her mouth demanding. Surprise surprise.

"Hey now. You'll get our dinner all sweaty."

■   ■   ■

"It would be good," China mentioned in the course of a mundane conversation with me, "if we got at some of my money soon."

Too many things needed to be resolved before Birdeye got out of Rack. Things can get heavy even in the simplicity of prison.

"Varney can't handle all my business on the street, you know—none of my people want to do business with an Anglo. And that's the way it should be." She waved a graceful arm at the racial slur. I assumed she excluded me from it. "She got more going on beneath the surface than the Mexico City sewers."

I thought China should check out her own self beneath the surface.

She showed me a letter from one of her home girls: The police were crazy, the girl wrote, wanting to know how she remembered the night Roland was killed, out of the hundreds of nights spent drunk in the bar; the police said it wasn't possible to remember that particular night, said she couldn't be sure China hadn't left the bar that night, that night, not some other night—"I said we were together all the time, China. I said: We even went to the bathroom together, man. But they don't want to hear it, you know?"

Her girlfriend was going back to Mexico City.

China told me I needed to find out who was pushing to reopen her case, terrifying her friends.

I didn't know how to do that. I didn't know how to tell her so.

"Then we know where the money is." China stood up, bracelets jingling, happy at the glum expression on my face. "Get us some, hey?"

■   ■   ■

China walked over to Control. "Hey, Claudia. When Birdeye comin' home?"

Claudia was on the phone, she shook her head at China. The voice on the other end, a rhythmic litany of complaint and accusations, droned; her face changed from the pale of shock to the slow glow of anger. "Oh shut up."

China nodded in sympathy, emotion was the currency of the day.

"I'll talk to you when I get home."

China wondered how she could speak so clearly through clenched teeth.

"Listen, shithead, somebody pays the bills, and it's me, so for God's sake leave me alone while I'm here. Leave me alone." Claudia threw the receiver down.

"Claudia, corazon, you don't love this man. Get rid of him." China reached over, plucked an emery board out of the pencil cup. She filed industriously. "I'm glad you're here because you're a nice woman, I like you, but it would be better if you weren't police, perhaps we could be real friends. Get rid of him."

The corrupted clarity of China's mind soothed Claudia. Men men men men. The end of the world. "You know, China, they can't all be losers." Claudia leaned back, crossed her legs. "It seems to me that there is something about a big cheerful, you know, built guy. You know, someone you'd like to watch with his shirt off."

"Oooh. Listen up, Claudia, you don't owe no man a free ride."

"Well. I hadn't taken it that far."

"Don't give it away now, Claudia."

"You know, I always feel better after seeing him. A funny kind of feeling—"

"That's love. It feels like you're gonna puke, huh? That's love." China was only trying to be helpful.

"I thought that was morning sickness." Rosalie staggered into the office, threw her greasy self on a chair. "Listen, Claudia. Write me a report. Tell them I've got something contagious. TB. Can't work in the cafeteria. Allergic to soap. Hello, China. Early morning air makes me crazy. Anything. Measles. You've got to get me outta there. It's hell."

China brushed her own shoulders and collar with the traditional "get lost" signs, but Rosalie sat unmoving like a huge lump of fat. China tried sarcasm, "It's not such a bad job. If you work a few more months you'll get moved up to the dish room."

Rosalie wondered if there was anyone in the whole damn place who didn't have a major bolt loose, her eyes began to glaze over, she was surrounded by creatures from another galaxy. "Claudia, get me an aspirin, huh?" She had to get out of the kitchen while she still could.

China ignored Rosalie. "Back there in Rack Birdeye's being frozen to death. Listen, Claudia, you've got to get her outta there before she gets sick."

Rosalie stirred herself. "Aspirin?"

China recognized a losing cause. She left. Rosalie continued to bleat as Claudia thought about quitting her job, moving to some island. Tropical.

• ELEVEN •

I stretched. Sitting in the cold law library chasing an elusive idea back through all the contradicting legal decisions and precedents, upheld and overturned, I'd stiffened up. My fingers were knotted around the pen, my knees creaked, I was a hundred years old.

I had tried to get some leverage out of the turkeys, an impossible task. The farm that supplied the prison lost their whole batch to the rains, yet here we were served turkeys anyway. Suspicions should be aroused behind a situation like that. But no one cared, lethargic conferences between the administration, the dietitian and the residents' council just used up the time. That's all. We'd be buried under turkey sandwiches, goddamn drowned turkey soup. Stagnant puddles, larvae.

China came in, a sweet diversion at last.

I asked her if she'd thought again about Rosalie.

"Yeah. Got to do something—I'm haunted by the picture of Birdeye suffering back in Rack."

"Birdeye should be out late today."

"Mmmm." China didn't sound pleased. "Just in time for drowned turkey dinner?"

Rosalie wandered in, something devious on her mind.

"Hey, Rosalie. Thanks for the invoices."

"I don't want to hear about those turkeys, okay?" Sullen. "What's the best method to get out of the cafeteria— besides suicide?"

"Listen, Rosie, you like men, right?" China fished in her pockets coming up with a couple different pills. "Here, swallow these. Much better than aspirin."

"What?" She absently popped two pills in her mouth. "Yeah. I like some men." She wasn't so sure which men she liked anymore, it seemed to her that men might not, as Birdeye put it, might not have enough places.

"No matter. I got a small problem with one of my runners. Maybe you'd like a visitor—wait! Don't get so suspicious. You seen him, tall thin light skin black dude, dresses real nice, was in visiting me last time your mother came in, remember?"

"No." She wondered what was it with everyone. Sex.

"Yes you do. He smiled at you, you smiled back."

"I must have been daydreaming."

"Well. He's my husband's brother."

Rosalie seemed to be trying to place the man.

"See. Birdeye is hot about my seeing Leonard, that's his name. He's noticed you in the visiting room, always asks about you. Oh, Rosalie, you must have seen him."

"So what?"

"So he wants to visit you, you guys can get something going, he bring you stuff, we cut you in. Oh, it'd be great. He really is a sweetheart."

Rosalie frowned.

"I've just got to make Birdeye feel secure about me. She'll kill herself, you know."

Rosalie thought things were coming across the plate a little too fast for her.

Since China was determined to do it, I figured I might as well get some licks in. "Rosalie, listen. We know you don't belong on closed custody—but you're yesterday's news, stuck back with the rabble. Might as well start to adjust to it." Ha.

I liked the sound: "Back with the Rabble." I chewed on it. "This visitor would pass the time for you. It may be a few weeks before you're out of the cafeteria unless this turkey thing gets rolling."

"I don't want to hear about those goddamn turkeys anymore!"

"Oh?"

"Just leave me out of the turkey thing, okay?"

Rosalie seemed to have more than a simple antipathy to turkeys. She leaned forward. "Listen, I think my career as a secretary is dead, Morgan. Cowboy seems pleased with that illiterate whore he's got up there now."

Rosalie started to take a cigarette from my pack, I moved it out of her reach. She acted as if it hadn't happened. "The bitch can't spell but she will spread her legs. Those fuckers will put me on janitorial next."

I knew better. Narcisse is never wrong about these things. Rosalie only had another week in the cafeteria, next re-class hearing she'd be out. "I didn't know you had such an aversion to honest labor."

"Damn straight. Easy is the job description I look for. Hey, I don't see you doing any floor scrubbing."

I looked at the debris underfoot. Rosalie was less charming every time I saw her. If she was going to submit herself to our manipulations she better keep a sharp eye on the negotiations.

China began to explain the setup. Fragments made it through the layers of Rosalie's self-absorption: bank books, interest rates, corporate accounts, it all made sense, but in some other context, not in prison, the realities were mutually exclusive.

"What's this?" She was trying to sound bright; like muscles all gone to flab, her voice showed no depth, she fumbled, "What are we talking about here anyway?"

China seemed absorbed in the cuff of her jeans.

"I suppose," awkward, "I should've been listening, I'm sorry. It's a new habit I've picked up in here, not listening, but it's only because no one says anything worth hearing. I mean, outside of my parole date I didn't think there was a thing anyone could say that I'd want to know about."

I explained, "That dead husband of China's, peace be on the dead, put some of their money in special accounts. A dummy company. Or two."

China didn't move.

I continued, suave, "Now no one out there can find the money. If it's not pulled out of those accounts soon, the bank will discover that our boy is dead, take all the money for their very own. Our China doll here will be up shit creek."

"Yeah?"

"This wonderful man, the brother of China's dead husband, claims he could make us all very wealthy women."

"Us? Oh my."

China spoke then, "Well sure. You visit with him, we count you in. After all, he got to be watched, I think he intends to make himself a wealthy man, leave us screw ourselves." Pretty. "But he be enough a fool we can use him. They's a lot of money involved here, I can't do it direct because of Birdeye, see?"

Rosalie scowled. "China, is this really the truth? It sounds so, well, involved."

"It is, rather." She shrugged. "There's Varney, my husband's mistress." China made a wry face. "She still work with me on the old real estate scam, keeping the front office open, collecting rents, sort of keeping things moving. A couple of other people take care of other stuff." Graceful shoulders completed the sentence, lift drop.

"Why so many people? So many banks? So many little games that don't add up?"

China looked concerned at Rosalie's lack of perception.

I wondered what happened to change China's scam from the forty-K cash money to bank bingo. I didn't much like groping my way through the dark labyrinths of China's plots, I decided to push. "It seems like everyone out there knows part of the story, no one knows the whole setup. China claims she knows less than anyone. This is not quite true, but she wants us to think so." Two can play the game. "China's the key to getting the money." I didn't take my eyes off Rosalie, knowing already what a nasty expression China was preparing for me. "I think she expects you to locate the lock."

Rosalie's mind was grinding, rusted gears struggling to turn, to talk money, like she was somebody. Her voice became firmer, "So why hasn't this Varney or somebody gone to the bank, got the money out?"

"They would have if they could have." China took a breath, "Leonard and Varney don't know where the right bank books are anyway."

"Tell us more."

"Varney still runs the property management company, we be like partners, you know?" Airy wave. "Some of the places we rent, we don't tell the main office, put the money in another account. Then there's always other stuff we be doin'. A lot is, you know, cash."

"Sounds like you're looking for answers to questions we can't answer in here."

"Well, Roland's dead and no one wants to do business with Varney. Legit or otherwise. You know? So. She's got a problem too. We all got to work together." China turned her great eyes on Rosalie.

I thought: We can't get there from here.

Rosalie didn't even try to refrain from condescension. "Well, I don't know enough about the general situation. What money? Cash? Bonds? I mean, where is it? Banks? Under some bed? Company accounts? Connected to other accounts? When was the last transaction? Who did it? How was it accomplished? Where are the bank books? Are we talking theoretically here or what?"

A slight edge, "What's in it for me?"

No answer.

"How much are we talking about here?"

China sat in silence, thinking perhaps that her money was going to be spread around like underwear in a whorehouse.

I remained silent too, doubting that any money existed.

Rosalie couldn't stop talking, "What's Leonard's part in all this? What's Varney doing now? Why won't anyone deal with her? Why aren't you answering?"

China seemed to be having trouble with her throat, her voice walked the borders, but I could see the dollar signs beginning to waver in Rosalie's eyes.

Patronizing, Rosalie recited the stats, "Payroll, company or cashier checks, with the amounts embossed on 'em are not too difficult to cash if they're under $2,500. Over that amount even company checks get serious scrutiny. Keep your checks below that amount, you can drain an account in one day going from branch to branch. If the checks are righteous."

She looked for another of my cigarettes, I let her find one this time. "Individual 'pay to bearer' checks are a much more difficult proposition. Banks hate to give it up, you know. So ideally you do it in $2,500 company checks, but if you must go higher you set it up so it was an insurance claim payment—those can be up to $7,500— more if it's well set up."

She waved the cigarette in a lecturing fashion. "A lot depends on the manner, how it's all presented. See, transfers over $7,500 get sent to the feds. I assume you'd rather not have them involved?"

China shrugged with apparent unconcern.

"You could do it by a big cashier check, if you could get one, hey—you can even do it with a phone call. Hell, I mean how much money do we have to move around— where do you want to put it?"

Rosalie didn't notice that China didn't answer, so wrapped up in her own speculations she could smell the money. "Bank books? Listen, honey, you don't need the book, just the numbers, transfer it somewhere else within the same banking system right over the phone. Or get someone with an ATM card hooked up to those accounts, I can dial it on a Touch-Tone phone up front. Do it just by pushing buttons."

Cut someone in, cut someone out. There wasn't enough money to make all the world happy. Hell. There couldn't be money enough in this scam to equal the complications. Besides it was playing havoc with my own schedule.

I pulled out the hooch jar, filled my cup to the brim, waved the jar at the two of them, but I didn't pour them one. They want hooch, they should earn it.

• TWELVE •

Cowboy was scowling as Johnson raved about the criminal population. Working on holidays. Saving the world from the depredations of the depraved. Nobody was interested in her sociology. To Narcisse, Johnson's lips seemed to form the word "sex sex sex" over and over again, slurping, but Narcisse supposed Johnson didn't have the courage to say it aloud.

Narcisse just finished fixing us a gourmet Thanksgiving dinner: roast lamb, sugar-baked yams, fresh-frozen peas. Salad, herb dressing. Apple pie. Cheddar cheese. The woman was a genius. She stowed it away in the plastic lining of her coat. Nodding at the guard she headed back to our cell. I was supposed to provide the liquor, even though Narcisse maintained that liquor was bad for people: "Alcohol's poison, Morgan. At least heroin isn't poison, it's just dangerous." I had put aside some of Birdeye's finest.

■   ■   ■

China and Rosalie left the law library still negotiating, I read my notes on China's case again. It was a shame that China hadn't solicited Tony the Loser to accidentally kill her husband. Or plea bargained the thing down to manslaughter conspiracy.

I always thought of these things.

Well, some sort of appeal, based on new evidence or procedural mistakes in the sentencing seemed the only way to get her out. Solicitation to commit murder got the same damn time as doing it. Even finding the actual murderer wouldn't help. It did not look promising.

I didn't like China's money game either. I figured the easiest way to get myself out of it was to get China out of jail, out of my immediate vicinity—an appeal bond perhaps, let her do her own damn banking. Let me go back to doing my own damn thinking.

The INS was so hot to deport people there should be a chance to get China deported back to Mexico, where the authorities had no reason to lock her up. But China had full American citizenship from that silly marriage to Roland Lee. There was a lesson in there somewhere.

It's beyond me why people hang on to useless secrets, why China had to make everything so complicated—perhaps Birdeye or someone was going to have to take care of her on the streets after all. If there was any money they should buy Birdeye a red sports car so she wouldn't have to be stealing them all the time.

Back and back again. My big plans, dismantled. Parts missing. It took so much energy just to keep everyone from spending all their time in Rack. Or the psych treatment unit. I remembered my own three-minute interview. The psychologist woman chewed her nails, picked her nose, played with her key ring, then she accused me of being a spy. Her report read in part: "a dangerous passive-aggressive sociopath with delusions of grandeur." I was still outraged.

If only we could be left alone to do our time, take care of business: make booze, smuggle drugs, play mailroom Russian roulette. Big fucking deal, the world isn't at stake here. We don't want nothing fancy. Do our time in peace. Comfort. A little dignity. They can't hear it. It's just the truth. Just the truth.

Johnson burst into the law library.

"I smell marijuana smoke! I smell it! You've gone too far this time, Morgan! You treat this place like it was your own office. Well, that's over now."

As if things weren't depressing enough.

Claudia trailed in her wake. "Don't look at me, Morgan. I'm just here to see that justice is served." The counselor didn't look pleased. Any number of things about her job just then appeared distasteful. Good. I hoped she would be reluctant to sort through the law library mess for incriminating evidence.

Johnson was breathing hard, tugging at her rubberized uniform. "Up." She barked, "Up and put your hands against that wall." She was an eager one, that's for sure.

I didn't move. Claudia sighed, "No good, Johnson. That's not necessary."

In the proper ritual manner Claudia intoned, "There's been a complaint lodged against you that you've been smoking marijuana in here. Is that true?"

"True that there was a complaint? How should I know?" My mouth was stiff. "For your information, I haven't been smoking no marijuana." Jaws locked, eyes hooded. James Cagney. I appalled myself sometimes.

Claudia tried to wave Johnson toward the piles of law books on the tables.

Johnson scowled, came in close, she didn't want to miss anything. She grabbed a couple grimy papers, rustled them, hoping to make me do something silly. Then she'd haul my ass off to Rack quick as could be. She tried righteous indignation. "Only an idiot would believe this mess served any purpose. Privileged correspondence! These lawyers you're so tight with—you all think you're so smart. At every stage—" Johnson became so enraptured with herself that she waved the pages in my face. "It's just a front for more crimes. This is nothing but garbage!"

I snatched them back, ashes smudging the air between us. "You wouldn't know privileged correspondence if you sat on it, you feeble-minded Okie."

Johnson stepped back, twisting her hands around each other, strangling.

I straightened myself up, took a long drag off the cigarette, left my hand by my mouth for an extra few moments, swallowed strongly. Still swallowing, I turned my back, swallowed again. Close, but the roach went down. For a moment it was as big as a car.

The veins started to jump on Johnson's forehead again.

"You should maybe see a doctor about that twitch, Johnson."

She made a grab for my arm. I could smell her sweat.

"Hey! You don't have the right to paw me. Nor to be gratuitously offensive, not to mention idiotic, in the course of your job."

It was all too many syllables for Johnson. "Don't you dare talk to me that way! Threatening! An officer! You can't talk to me that way! I won't stand for it! You can't talk to me that way!"

I disengaged myself, moved a step away, I didn't feel like being slobbered on by some acrid smelling creep. Narcisse poked a worried face around the doorjamb; I shrugged, indicating it seemed to be all right so far. Next time I looked she was gone.

Claudia got another one of those insights she tried so hard to avoid, all this trouble and emotion over something unimportant. There was no evidence of marijuana usage, I was never even peripherally associated with drugs. There was no reason, except for Johnson's bizarre insistence, to be in there.

Claudia bustled around between us, nervous, rapid. "We're not here to discuss points of law now, ladies. Please both of you just stand there and don't talk to each other anymore, I can't stand to hear two intelligent women," I didn't correct her, "talking nonsense."

She opened a desk drawer, looked inside. Shut it. Opened another. Shut it. Methodical. She went through my desk, wondering aloud how anyone could run a law office in such utter chaos.

Out of the corner of my eye I could see Johnson start to do a kind of Lamaze breathing, change colors. If Johnson were to throw up in the law library it would be one hell of a mess.

Claudia passed over my hooch jar and glasses without a pause.

Claudia wiped her hands. "The desk has been

searched. Officer Johnson, will you look through the wastepaper baskets?"

"I will not." She didn't become a policewoman for that.

"Morgan, why can't you keep a cleaner office?"

I just lifted my eyebrows. We going to talk neat now?

Claudia smiled small. "Okay. We assume there is no contraband in the trash." Brisk. "We find no contraband in the desk. Nor on the person."

"Hey! You didn't search her! I'll give her a good search."

Claudia repeated in her calmest voice that that would not be necessary. I thought about insisting, now that I was clean, but I didn't want to intrude.

Johnson turned a full circle in exasperation, like a fat child. "I'm going to make a full report on both of you. But you!" She waved a pudgy finger in Claudia's face. "Your attitude is beyond understanding! You're derelict in your duties, fraternize in a manner unbecoming to our uniform." I could smell her sweat. "This has been going on for too long."

"Let's go, Johnson." Claudia turned away from her subordinate. Johnson was like those awful little animals whose only defense was puking something disgusting all over their attackers.

Too damn bad Johnson hadn't been forced to sweep up the floor for evidence. With her tongue.

■　　■　　■

I had made amphetamines in my bloodstream from caffeine, nicotine and rage; entering our cell I signed to Narcisse, "No hooch tonight. That fat fucker Johnson tried to bust me."

Narcisse patted a place on the cot next to her, held out her arms to me, I collapsed next to her. Her hands drifted to the badge position on her chest then curled rudely under her chin, an appropriate closeness in meaning be-

68   *LOW BITE*

tween the two words it signified: dirty and pig. "Officer Johnson thinks we're all criminals." Winking. "I knew you'd get out of it, you looked very relaxed when I saw you."

I seldom could tell when she was sarcastic.

She put a hand up to her forehead as if putting on a hat, made smooth motions marking a mustache, a handsome face (Narcisse was not unaware of Cowboy's odd charm). "Cowboy and Johnson were into sex earlier today."

It was easy enough for me to misinterpret what Narcisse said.

Narcisse imitated Johnson talking, small obscene irrelevant sounds came out as her mouth moved, "Sex sex sex sex sex." She puckered her smiling lips.

"Johnson," I made the nasty under-the-chin gesture, "is the most disgusting piece of shit on the planet." My awkward finger spelling scarcely distorted the meaning at all. I wondered again at our ability to talk this way.

She handed her cup to me with lazy drifting hands, graceful as slow-motion photography. I drained it, no reason for me to stand around buzzing in frustration while Narcisse had the comfort of technicolor. "Where's dinner?"

Narcisse pointed to the ceiling grate.

We stretched out on the bunk letting every muscle go slack, ideas rotated color-filled through our minds; we curled up together listening with our skin, the way people do who can't hear.

Celestial applause.

• THIRTEEN •

Birdeye got out of Rack late that afternoon. Thanksgiving. But her thanks and pleasure were contaminated by all the thinking she'd done in Rack: "Listen to me, China, I can't have you fucking around on me."

China lifted her head out of a nod, half-smiling. "Hummm?"

"I'm referring to that doped-up brother-in-law of yours."

"I told you, Birdeye. He's gonna visit Rosalie now."

"He still got you on the string."

"No no—I've got him on the string." Musing, "Maybe use that string to hang him."

"Explain yourself, girl."

"Well, Leonard sort of been pushin' at me, you know? He's not handlin' our business right. See, I think Roland turned the money over twice the night he was killed. Had put some of it into checks that night." China settled into the pillows, pulled Birdeye back into the circle of her arm. "I found out about it on the side, so to speak, went by the office, just to make sure I got my cut."

"He try cut you out often?"

"Every time. Anyway, I came up quiet, looked in the window. Roland was on the couch with his head all blown off, Leonard standin' over him."

"I knew he was a wrong one! Blow away his own brother."

"I don't think so, Roland was long dead by then; besides, Leonard woulda took the money." China wondered how elaborate she'd have to make her story. "But he don't have it. I checked."

"You checked?" Birdeye hooted, unconvinced. "Well, were you alone?"

"For sure. People thought I'd just stepped outside the bar to score or something."

"I don't like this." Birdeye moved away. "You coulda took that money your ownself. Killed him. Now you got everyone looking for that money just so you can watch them run around. Keep everyone dis-tracted while you and Leonard plan how to spend it." Birdeye stood up, her little face pinched. Hostile. "No. I don't like this at all. My old lady should show, has got to show, more class."

"Class? Class? Where you get this shit? I *got* class, sweet-heart!" China got up too, standing nose to nose. "I got more class in my little finger than most of these bitches got in their whole fucking bod-ees."

Birdeye moved toward the door, out of reach. "You for-get, China, I know you. I know you."

Birdeye joined the crime mob in the rec room.

China floated in a few moments later.

Birdeye hunched over the cards. Serious business.

"Come on, play, turkey."

"Don't talk to me about it, girl."

"We going for supper or what?"

"Not on your life."

"Come on, nigger, get up off that deuce." Gold mine fortunes riding on each hand.

"Oh but no—if I do got it here in this hand, now you know more than I do. You livin' in the past, darlin', that was last hand."

"The only reason you got it was she was dealin'."

"Girl knows cards."

"Well, Thanks-giv-ing be done by tomorrow, they move on to some other thing—"

"Still gone be turkey. They's lots of it."

China got up from the folding chair she'd pulled up behind Birdeye. Her tentative offer of a back rub had been shrugged off; she stretched her legs a little, wandered over to the record player. "Hey girl, play some Al Green."

"That's all you ever want to hear."

"Okay, Jerry Butler then. Ice Man gone be senator someday." China took a couple smooth steps, turned it into a fancy bump and grind, started to hum. The record started.

"Hey listen, girl, I can't concentrate on these cards with you wigglin' around."

China pulled herself up short for a count of three, pouting, at least Birdeye was talking to her. Big Deal. "Don't look then." Slow shoulder shimmy walk.

"For Christ sake, Birdeye, look what you done here— you fucking threw that Jack away. Your ass is mine, girl."

China slinked across the room, hitting all the turns, sliding into a little grapevine, then back into the basic moves. Two other women just out of the shower joined in, moving together with a ripple snake step, white towels wrapped around their heads: The Tropitones on a special tour from Vegas dropped in to entertain the girls tonight.

Birdeye lost the hand badly. Her partner grieved. Birdeye apologized with a dignified shrug, cast a cold eye at the dancers. "Not my style. You know what I mean?"

"Look, Birdeye, sounds like a family affair. Maybe you should keep it that way?"

"Keep it all in the family like? Sure. That's what I should do. Keep it all in the family." She stood up. "I'm history. Find yourself someone else."

China would have followed her out but The Tropitones were into one of those intricate three-person spin around step forward arm extended hip snap left and right, she couldn't break it up. She was off anyway so they called it quits.

China shared some nachos with the rest of The Tropitones. "Last supper."

"Bet there's better food in Rack."

"Birdeye didn't seem to think so."

Everyone knew there'd be some change, we just didn't know if we'd starve to death before it came.

■   ■   ■

The next day China and Rosalie walked to the visiting room together. Dressed to kill. Rosalie hissed, "Tell me more about this guy Leonard. And quit fussing."

China ran a quick comb through her hair, pouted at her reflection in the door glass, twitched her ass, winking. "Well Rosalie, he's a real good dancer, used to set up dance routines for professionals, you know, like strippers. Was on a tour with this exotic dancer in Mexico City, that's how I met him. You know."

Rosalie didn't know.

"He introduced me to his brother—Roland was a little more handsome, a lot more, you know, straight seeming. Leonard isn't very, well, straight. But he's real smart. Reads a lot. Science fiction. Psychology. Been driving a bus for the city down here, he's good people. You'll see."

Lily, nodding as if she were part of the joke, tango-danced like a heavy polar bear cub behind them. As they approached the entrance Lily twirled around, said, "Okay bye," zipped behind a tree where she could watch everything almost without being seen.

I positioned myself at the table next to China's, smiled at the intense law student sitting across from me, and proceeded to ignore her. I shouldn't have been so brusque that day, she was a charming girl, and I could have used her help. But my mind wasn't with her.

China's Leonard was tall, dark, fine-featured, California curled, blatant in his survey of the room, sniffing the hothouse air, lingering over the female flesh around him. "Hey, China, I got some change—want a soda or something from the machine?"

China didn't look my way, just watched Leonard move between the tables. It was a dangerous game she was trying to play. She told me later that she had second thoughts, but Birdeye—

Leonard was going to check in with her once in awhile, to keep her informed. "To make sure he's not rippin' me off too badly. Some I expect, it's not too much to pay for peace in the family, but more than that," China grimaced, dramatic finger across throat, "I'll cut him quick as shit."

This time, she said, if he played her for the fool she'd be professional about it. No hired help, she was learning all sorts of things in prison.

She dimpled at him as he returned with the sodas, asked him how he liked the view. "Not too bad. I like that type. Built for comfort, you know? Lush. The mother's not too bad either. Maybe I'll chat her up when she's leaving. Offer her a ride—do you suppose she came on a bus? What's the family money like anyway? You find out?"

"Oh hell, Leonard, leave Rosalie's mother out of this, okay? Rosa's in on some straight beef. She's a very straight lady, Leonard, so be straight with her. She doesn't know anything much about the life."

"Say now that's real fine. I'd like to learn more about that straight stuff—think she teach me? We could use someone like that. What you think?"

"Leonard. Come on. Just take it one step at a time, quit trying to make it more elaborate than it already is."

Their eyes reflected a mutual understanding. I was getting a distinct feeling about all this. I didn't like it.

There was something vague, reptilian, about this smooth good-looking man. The winter sunlight played on his hands, long clever lazy fingers. I watched them closely; he may once have been China's lover, but it must have been a long time ago, there was little heat generated between them.

Rosalie looked at him with rabbit eyes.

"Hey. Whatever it is you better tell me about it." Her mother fixed Rosalie in her X-ray vision. "I'll find out soon enough, you know."

Rosalie shrugged. Tough. "Ahhh, Ma, just fighting the pressures of doin' time. I got involved in a little thing the other night. I'm working in the kitchen for awhile instead of doing secretarial up front."

"What little thing! Between you and your sister I'll just go mad. What have I done wrong as a mother? Tell me, Rosalie, it won't kill me. Not yet anyway."

Her mother was very good at these things. "No, Mamma, you'll live forever, we won't always be such a burden. We're, like, going through a phase, you know?"

"Heee-ey, Rosalie, come over. Say hello."

Rosalie went all pale, then red, her thin voice wobbled, "Hey, China's here? We should go say hello? I bet he's a veteran, hey Ma? Whaddaya think?"

Her mother trailed along, kissed China on the cheek, they murmured together for a moment, then she turned her gaze on Leonard. She stiffened, became rather brisk in her movement, shook hands. Rosalie shook hands rather longer than was necessary, he let his eyes go deep with promises. I wondered if he was as obvious as he seemed.

Leonard was standing now, turning on the charm, but her mother looked up at him as if he were some strange bug; Rosalie moved through glue.

It wasn't as if they could just sit down, bullshit for a minute, then say, "Oh well, let's blow this place, it's too dull for us." Leonard rumbled at Rosalie with a voice as smooth as cream sherry. The man in the Black Velvet ad. Rosalie let the sound roll around her head, ripple down her back.

She tried to get down to business. "How long have we known each other, where did we meet?"

"In heaven, lovely lady. In heaven. We've known each other for lifetimes. You know how you can recognize family even before you've been introduced? Well that's what happened when I saw you. I'm so glad," he took her hand again, "that you're tight with my little sister here." The man presented this shit as if it were original.

Rosalie tried to be sensible. "No, man. For the visiting request. We have to have our story straight." Her mother was looking up from her conversation with China.

"Right, right. Two years."

"Okay by me. We meet in LA? On a bus you were driving?" That sounded practical.

"Wow, man. How unromantic. I thought maybe I could just fall down at your feet, worship a little when you were buying lingerie or something."

Rosalie's mouth tightened. He didn't seem to focus on how important it was to get this set up. Time was running out. The visiting room guard was on his way over. Rosalie stood up, "Come on, Mamma, our coffee's almost cold, we got family to rake over the coals."

"Oh yes of course, dear. Now China, you remember what I told you. You got to take care of yourself. Take at least 500 milligrams of vitamin C every day." They walked back to their table chatting.

"Vitamin C? She mean cocaine, huh, little girl?"

China let her eyes rest in speculation on his handsome face for a long moment. "Still into it, hey, Leonard? Can't put the pipe away."

"Now listen here, little girl. You know I hate it when people jam me up, I got it under control now. Musta been a week or ten days."

"I bet you got the friggin' pipe in your shoulder bag, you freak."

He laughed, self-pleased. "Well yes. I couldn't help it. I love to tease these people, I know they'd never find it. I got ways. Ways to distract people when they search through my stuff, you know. I got ways." He smirked, reached into his pocket for cigarettes, a lighter, handed them to her, she fumbled with them, lighting one for each of them. While handing his over, she stood up, slid one hand into her pants, pushed a bullet-shaped balloon up inside herself.

"Let me do it next time, okay?"

"Go fuck yourself, Leonard." Casual. She'd said it to him a hundred times.

My unproductive interview was coming to an end. We shook hands, I left the room, loitered outside with Lily.

China and Rosalie walked past us, recovering from the pressures of dealing with the free world. "So listen, it went pretty smooth, huh? You like him, huh? Just like I said, huh?"

Rosalie heard mermaid voices. "Oh. Yeah. Sure. What the hell."

• FOURTEEN •

"So what else you want me to do, Morgan?"

Alexander distracted me by his mere presence, he poked in my book rubble, shuffled his feet in my debris; he was suntanned in December, glowing with that scratchy male energy, tired of being ignored, annoyed because he saw no way out of it. Again. What did he expect? A blow job? I said, "How could you let that editor tell you 'turkeys aren't news after Thanksgiving'?"

"It's not my goddamn fault, Morgan. Jeez." He continued pacing, I continued watching.

"First," a collegiate lecturing tone, "you ask me to set up an appeal for China, I don't tell you I think you're chasing invisible bugs, no, I say sure, I'll work on it. Then when I bring you something, all you fucking talk about are the goddamned turkeys. No one cares about the stupid turkeys, Morgan."

"Poor boy. Shouldn't dress so fine to come to this crummy place. Hang around with criminals. A nice boy like you. Does your grandmother know you're here?"

His eyes sparked with frustration. "You haven't even looked at the damn thing yet." He tossed it at me. "I mean, it wasn't an easy thing to do, I can't pick locks like you, or blast the door halfway to hell. We're talking the administration's files here."

Cool as a river, "I never blasted any door to hell."

"So come on. Tell me what you want your little servant here to do for you now? How about the key to Fort Knox?"

"Doesn't have a key."

He turned away, his arms in a "praise heaven" pose. He did it very well.

"Odd." I poked at the rap sheet as if it were a small turd. "No, man, this is all wrong. No arrests? No tickets? No nothing?"

Alexander waited.

"I've seen him. That man done some time, Alexander. Nobody is this clean. Either someone got to this—well, come on, Alexander, what's the deal here?"

"Describe Leonard to me."

"Sleezeball. Scumbag. But handsome, don't get me wrong. In a weird way."

"Give it to me straight. Height, weight, you know."

I took it slow. "He's something over six feet, skinny. No shit. Hey, China's Leonard and this Leonard aren't the same guy."

"I said I'd double-checked, this is the sheet on Leonard."

"So who the hell is the man in the visiting room?"

He smirked. "It'll be at least a week before I can get a copy of Roland's stats from the basement at City Hall. They don't keep dead people with the active ones."

"Yeah. Sure. Lovely. Leonard's not the walking dead, Alexander."

Smug. "Roland was listed as missing before he turned up dead."

"No shit." I looked up from the sheet. "Hey. Turn around, you fuckhead. I can see you grinning to your wretched self over there. Get over here, help me think. Damn."

"Taken off missing persons after he died. A couple months after."

"Stop pacing around, you make me crazy. We've got work to do."

He shook his head at me. "I feel something terrible coming on."

"No no. Come on over here, sit down."

I cleared a space in the debris, placed two clean glasses on the desk. There was no way I was going to work it if he remained on full alert. I lifted my glass, "To Leonard. Whoever the hell he is."

This batch was from apples, sort of a jailhouse Calvados. Birdeye's idea. "I figured I should give you a taste.

It's been going through some improvements." Alexander seemed to appreciate it.

Good to have a drink handy for times like these. Alexander was smart. He was pretty. Even so, I hated his invasion of my life, his assumption of control. "Leonard wasn't even called in for questioning behind his brother's death? No statements? No nothing?"

Alexander concentrated, sipping. "Apparently not. If there was anything else in Leonard's file up front, my contact didn't see it. She said she'd copied everything that she found."

"Maybe your connect didn't know what she was doing." I motioned him closer, did some serious talking. He looked interested, dubious, hostile, insulted, sullen, then bullied into agreeing. He did not look pleased.

"You can do it, Alexander. You can do it easy. I'm sure he's every bit as fond of boys as he is of girls."

He made indignant noises. I poured again. Sober he'd never agree.

"Just remember to keep your pants on, sweetheart."

"Jesus, Morgan. You're sick."

Another glass. He leaned in close. "You don't like me, do you, Morgan?"

"Uhn." I breathed in the expensive smell of him. I liked him. A useless piece of information.

"Shit." He slammed his glass down. "You're some broad, Morgan. I've never met anyone like you."

"I've met too many people like you." Stony.

"What's that supposed to mean?"

"Rich, pretty, smart. You're on some schoolboy lark in here, into some kind of sociological study or something. It's all a big game, isn't it now?"

"No. Where'd you get this shit?" His voice cracked like an adolescent. I liked that.

"I'm here to tell you—I mean I'm locked in here—Imagine trying to entertain yourself in an area no bigger than a football field. Can't you get it through your head: I don't get to leave, I don't get—I don't get to choose what

I'll do tomorrow. What I'll eat or who I'll see or when I'll get up or where I'll be or what I can think or say or do."

"I didn't mean—"

"Listen, Alexander. I need that information. It's not for some little scam, Alexander. It's not that I want to humiliate you or some shit. I need that information. You are the only one who can get it." I would do anything to make him get it. "You. You are invulnerable: If you ever got in trouble, Daddy could buy you off." I thought about that. "Hell, you have enough money to buy your own self off."

I worked on his liberal guilt, supposing that he had some. Another cigarette, another swallow. "There's nothing anyone can do about it. It's the way the world is. So I use you. While I can." I didn't look at him, having gone beyond what I meant to say. I played it softer. "I am sorry."

"You're raving, Morgan," he was smiling. He must have thought this was good: me apologizing. "Answer the question."

"Oh, Alexander. I like you very much."

He thought he was gaining ground here.

"But that is irreverent. Irrelevant." I never lost control. "I've tried to keep an open mind about you, you know."

"The suspense has been killing me."

"Me too. But that's all right. It builds character." I watched with approval as his face took on a smug drunken shine.

He wondered if anyone ever died from hooch.

"Sure. That's the chance you take. One year some dumbfuck used wood alcohol. Knocked off a couple people." I took a breath. Push him. "Could happen any time. What'sa matter, you wanta live forever?"

There was time. Plenty of time. Swordplay. Still fencing, feinting, thrusting, thriving on suppression. I gave him the full voltage.

Before he left he sucked on a handful of mints. He had to go teach a class.

• FIFTEEN •

Claudia and her God-besotted husband were having screaming fights over the phone right in the unit. The man gave everything a biblical explanation; she said it was a good thing God talked to him, she certainly wasn't going to. She suggested that he move out, take God with him, he refused. The man was certifiable, she said, but she was afraid of the complications involved with committing him to some nuthouse. People couldn't just dump husbands off like at Goodwill: Here, this one's broken.

Divorce? Desertion? Murder? What, she asked me, was the difference between a mortal sin and a venial sin anyway? What would she do without a husband? Everybody's got to have one?

She didn't know what to do, she was getting crazy herself.

We avoided her as much as possible.

■　　　■　　　■

Turkeys don't know enough to get in out of the rain, let alone fly out of the rising puddles. Like convicts. Rosalie believed her life would always be this endless stream of filthy pots, soapy water, elaborate plots for petty crimes. Living the life of the desperation regulars she leaned on the metal sink in the dim blue lights of the cafeteria, staring at the wall of oversized stainless steel utensils bowls spatulas serving forks spoons, no knives, but still an infinity of useful tools. Each one washed by hand. Her hand.

"Deuce is crazy, you know?" Thea threw pots around with lethal abandon. "She never takes off that bloody apron—the blood of her victims. She even sleeps in it."

"What do I care? I'm not sleeping with her."

"Don't come wailin' to me if you wake up dead."

Rosalie tossed her head, went over to talk with Deuce, but she couldn't keep her eyes off the bloody apron; when she returned to the sinks Thea had disappeared.

She hefted a pot, grumbling now she'd have to do all the work herself, watched her muscle flex. She made an experimental fist, it might be nice to punch somebody. She'd never punched anyone. On further thought, she'd probably get killed.

Queenie came by searching for Thea. Subliminal Siamese twins: Their self-involvement was total, consuming. Made normal social intercourse difficult, Rosalie was pleased they hadn't killed her yet. They told her they were trying to make a bomb. Going to blow up the administration building, she shouldn't be in any hurry to go back to work up there.

They were also into smaller terrors.

Officer Claudia threaded her way through the morning chaos, round-shouldered with her own problems, she made it unscathed back to the sinks, handed Rosalie a visiting room slip. "Visitor for Miss Rosalie."

"Who is it?"

"Now, girl, I surely don't know. Think you'd be glad anyone come visit you; with your attitude I'm surprised anyone at all bothers; I bet you can't remember when was the last time you took your nose out of your own ass."

Claudia wasn't supposed to work that day, but it seemed better than staying home. She couldn't remember why anymore. As Claudia walked away she said to herself, "No more understanding than a banana," very quiet. She liked it so much she said it again. "Bunch of self–centered little whores in here anyway."

Queenie came right over. "What's up?"

Thea, who had not been seen in ten, fifteen minutes, stuck her head out of the pot steamer machine. "Claudia says that Rosalie is full of herself."

Queenie grabbed Thea by the scruff. "I told you not to go in there when I'm not around. Some damn fool will turn it on, you be Kentucky steam-fried nigger." She pulled Thea out like a squirming turtle from its shell.

"Steam your own self. I turned the steam cock off." Thea shook herself loose from the taller woman's grip, confided to Rosalie, "Was checking it out for a guillotine. Never thought to just push someone in and steam 'em. Person couldn't even hear 'em scream."

Rosalie choked.

"Here it was right in front of me, I never noticed." She chirped, "Queenie has better perceptions, cut straight to the bone every time."

Rosalie backed away, swallowing the fear spit that collected in the corners of her mouth.

They watched her graceless exit, their arms looped around each other, grinning. Rosalie never knew what genuine pleasure she gave them; Thea and Queenie hadn't met anyone as dumb as Rosalie in a long, long time.

Rosalie figured she'd be called to work up front again just in time to be blown up, or else Cowboy would call for her too late, after she'd already been steamed to death. Headless.

She saw Leonard speed-rapping at the visitor's desk, rolling his eyes at the cop, ducking his head, flirting in the phoniest way. The man seemed whacked out beyond Saturn. She shuddered.

He hugged her. As they sat he tossed a wad of gum or something to ricochet off the back wall into a garbage sack. He bounced in his chair, pleased as a child.

"Hey baby, here I am. Sweeten your life." He lit her a cigarette. "Have you missed this man huh? Hope you been dreaming about him." He leaned in, kissed her hair. There was a strong smell of detergent. "Like he been dreamin' about you."

This was an important visit for Leonard. Time to put the wheels in mo-tion. This soapy smelling girl had to be pulled into line fast or it was all going down the tubes. He couldn't let that happen—he didn't like to waste time.

"So what do you girls do in here anyway, I mean do you rub up against things often or is it mostly tongues well hey baby lips teeth tongue I'm a pro a past master, if you want something to rub up against—" He ran a warm finger up the inside of her arm.

Rosalie's first visit alone with Leonard seemed to be two people having a conversation with two other people entirely: "So where do you do your banking? I might know the place? I used to hang around banks a lot, you know?"

He didn't seem interested in banks. He played with a strand of her hair.

"Nice of you to find time out of your busy schedule to visit, Leonard."

"Hey baby, here, give me your hand."

She discovered that she had a handful but it wasn't all that exciting. He was annoyed. She apologized. He said well just keep on holding on, let me reach around in here. She moved away. He was annoyed again.

He smiled at Johnson who had been hovering around their table. Rosalie sucked a cigarette down to nothing. Lit another, filter end. It was awful.

He brushed his hand across her back, trailing his fingers along her spine, gratified to see her shiver.

Officer Johnson stood over the garbage sack, pointing to it, daring Cowboy to reach in, find out what Rosalie's black pimp threw in there.

Leonard was oblivious to the impending crisis. "Watch this now." He switched cigarette packs with a movement so deft Rosalie wouldn't have noticed if he hadn't cued her. He couldn't bear not to have an audience, smiling so close his breath ruffled her hair. "Hang on to this pack, don't open it til you're home. I put some important stuff in there, girl. I spent some time with Varney, you know, our old partner."

Rosalie didn't know. Didn't care. She wondered how much longer she would have to stay in the visiting room.

"Cleaned her apartment for her. Nice girl, but greedy, you know?"

Rosalie maintained a discreet silence, let her mind drift.

Leonard had not cleaned the apartment so much as cleaned it out, but it was all the same to him. He felt it was time to make some quick moves. He had taken a commuter flight north, stepped out into the icy winds of San Francisco. Pulling at the collar of his thin jacket he wondered how he'd managed to forget the lousy weather. He'd misspent his youth in the Mission district—had no friends or fond memories from that time, remembering only that he was the odd man out in the family, an unrecognized genius. He read psychology books so he knew how difficult it was for people with ordinary minds to appreciate his. He was scowling by the time he got on the bus next to a round overperfumed woman. He lit a cigarette, blew the smoke at his reflection in the window. The driver told him to put it out or he could take his black ass off the bus. Warm, welcoming San Francisco.

The downtown station on Ellis Street was strictly lowlife. Since the cold weather kept most of the people indoors at night, the only witnesses to his arrival were some lurkers snickering in doorways as he stalked by still scowling. Nothing ever slipped into the groove.

"I went up north to talk to Varney. But the girl never where she should be. Just for an example, when Roland got aced, where was she? Zoned out standing right over him. Staring. The whore has timing like no one's business." He said it took some quick thinking to get her away so he could look for the money. He was real glad she wasn't the hysterical type. He didn't find the money right then, he said, opening his eyes real wide to let her know there was more to the story.

Rosalie pursed her lips. Money.

"The first suspect in these things is always the other woman, it looked like Varney was a discarded mistress." Leonard drew the scene for Rosalie: If the police knew she'd been there it would have looked like a revenge killing. "But," he said, "I never told them—Varney was just a very unlucky girl, in the wrong place at the wrong time.

I got her out of there before phoning the police."

"You phoned the police?"

"Well, after awhile. They got to show up sometime. When I finished my business, they could paw him over all they want."

Roland had just collected big, simultaneous scores: a month's rent on an empty warehouse and the turnover from a couple ounces of junk. But Leonard came up empty when he searched the place.

They sighed simultaneously.

The money had to be somewhere: the office, the apartment. Somewhere. "That tightwad Roland never put it in the safe or nothing, just hid it up in one place for awhile, then moved it somewheres else. Didn't even trust his own brother."

Leonard took Rosalie's hand in his. "Varney just looks at me dumb whenever I try to question her, she doesn't seem to know what I mean. But I kept her on the line, just in case one day she wanted to talk about it. Trying to push Varney, except in person, is a waste, she just fade off into the middle distance."

Rosalie couldn't see that any of this shit was going to make her rich.

Leonard said that when God made red hair he must have done something with the soil it grows in, like the brain matter itself was not fertile or something. "I counted on those long strong thighs of hers to keep me warm up there in San Francisco." He mumbled a little in regret. It seemed that as soon as he was gone she just as happily forgot about him. He suspected that most of the women he fondly thought of as his had the same unfortunate lapse. It was something in the way women's minds worked. Immediate gratification. Even China, who should be grateful beyond eternity that he graced her grubby existence with his visits, seemed unimpressed.

Which is why he wanted Rosalie.

She looked easy. Just about ready to fall over behind that tough face she pulled on. If he got her wanting it bad enough he figured he'd ream his way into her own bit of stash. Fat City. No more "Justaminit Leonard, I don't wanna do that." It'd be all his way. The right way. About time, he was due.

Leonard shifted postures to let his cock slide against his thigh, always a reassurance. His sexual prowess was the bottom line; he arranged a lock of Rosalie's hair, let his hand linger as her eyes warmed up. He was gratified to see her relax, lean into his hand. He'd take her down too, she'd beg him for it. Beg him.

"Well, darlin', I've been dreaming about licking you all over. I've got plans and plans."

Hope and greed played tag across Rosalie's wide face. She chewed a piece of candy bar. Didn't say anything.

He gritted his teeth, changed tactics. Played it the young boy, timid, unsure. When he got masterful on her it would be irresistible. He opened his eyes wide, peered up through his lashes, seeming entranced by her grinding jaws. "You know, sometimes it seems as if fate played a big part in our meeting."

She raised her eyebrows at him.

No sensitivity to nuance. Leonard thought innuendo went right by most white broads anyway. Maybe past sisters too. He wasn't all that secure about sisters—they seemed to look at him once, then erase him. Made it difficult to get over with them. "Come on, loosen up, you're just as tight-wound as a girl on her first date. Now listen, I finally got a line going on China's checks."

Rosalie sat up straighter, her eyes glowing. Money.

Both of them had an inflated idea of their own abilities, each underestimating the depths to which the other would sink, given a reason to do so.

Their heads bent closer together.

"Found them when I shook down Varney's apartment."

The plan had gotten elaborate, medieval. Complicated beyond his ability to control. He smiled his favorite slo-mo grin at her, ducked his head. "We gone be rich. I'm gonna do right by China." His hand moved like a caress across her back, he leaned over her. "By you too, baby."

He began a discreet nibbling at her ear. "But time is of the essence as they say, you know?"

Johnson stomped over, Cowboy strolling a few steps behind, taking it all in. The guard proclaimed, "This man is intoxicated. Trying to pass contraband. This visit is terminated."

Rosalie sat rigid in her chair as the high color faded from her cheeks. People stopped talking, drilled her with their eyes. Cowboy stood with his arms folded, one of his what-will-you-do-now expressions. Waiting.

Johnson, rubbing her hands together, said Rosalie was going to be taken back to the clinic area, where a nurse was waiting to give her an internal. She waved a greasy wad of paper from the garbage sack. "This will be written up in your file."

Rosalie looked at the wad of paper, took her hand off the cigarette pack.

Leonard stood up to give Cowboy a jazz rap about how there's no law against young love, how he didn't do anything wrong. How he'd been so lonely for this lovely girl. La di and la da.

Rosalie wanted to die.

Every time Cowboy had seen his erstwhile secretary in the last two weeks she had been involved in something scandalous. He made up his mind to save her from the life she was getting into, pictured to himself what sweet salvation was in store, but confronting this newest aberration, he wondered if it was going to be worth it.

• SIXTEEN •

I felt bleary, like a mother whose children were all a big disappointment. I fumbled around in my desk drawer looking for a cigarette. Lily came side-shuffling into the law library, fiddling with the buttons on her shirt, too large for her now that the Thorazine fat was burning off.

"Hey? You hear yet?"

"Uh?" I was not feeling bright.

"I know all about it, I know all kinds of things, Morgan. But I won't say anything to anyone else. Just you. Unless of course I get some kind of guarantee. I'm no fool."

I put my smoke down, got sad right in the pit of my stomach. Had she come in this deranged—was it jail, the nut ward, what? Is attempted murder a sign of something irreparable? Desperation? Madness? Is there a difference?

"That man is filled with evil, Morgan." She drew herself up. "Hungry, just like his brother. Nothin' ever fill him, nothin' ever satisfy, the hunger has 'im. That's why he kills." Solemn.

I hadn't the foggiest.

"Nobody ever see me when I listen in. I don't belong in here, do I, Morgan?"

"No, you don't belong here. Nobody belongs in here, Lily, but here we are. Like your blessed drowned turkeys." I was careful. "That a big secret you have, huh?"

"I used to be pretty, you know. But my hair got all stringy back there, and I grew. Oh how I grew. You wouldn't believe how I grew."

Lily looked in all the corners of the room, approached me whispering, "I thought Cowboy was gonna belt Leonard but all he did was toss him out the visiting room, send Rosalie back to the nurse for an internal. Hey. Leonard, he stands there in the parking lot talking to himself, waving his hands around. Like he was nuts."

Lily nodded in satisfaction. "Just steaming as he got on the bus."

"The bus? Alone?"

Lily looked at me as if I were the one who was nuts. "Course. Who you think he be with? His brother?" Lily thought about this, head tilted to one side, looking for the joke. "Well, he did kill his own brother, you know. So like that, he carries him around with him everywhere: metaphysics. Is that what you meant?"

Oh hell. That wasn't what I meant. I didn't know what I meant. Except that Leonard would fuck his brother's wife, but not kill him. Takes a certain mindset to blow off someone's head.

The situation deteriorated.

Rosalie steamed into the law library, followed closely by China who was sweet voiced, cajoling. "Aw, c'mon. Give 'em to me, Rosalie, they're mine." At the sound of her voice the individual hairs on my forearms rose up.

Rosalie stuttered, "They're mine. I got 'em through Customs. Fucking Cowboy waited around to find out if I came up clean. Does he think some nurse poking around inside me with a rubber finger is exciting?"

China eyed me in mute appeal. Busy little law practice I had all of a sudden. I felt a certain amount of pity for Rosalie, not much; I tried to sound intelligent, "There are people that are just garbage, Rosalie. All people aren't worth the same, except perhaps in a philosophical sense: Like all of life is a manifestation of some divine spark—"

Rosalie wondered aloud how come I could never stay on one subject.

I was starting to have a good time. Oratory had a certain attraction. I pushed on, "On a practical level—the one we live, dream, work on—things roll along to their destination, no matter what we do. Our actions, maybe even our existence, are totally irrelevant." I gave a gracious pontifical wave. "Generally the thing is mutual, even though everything seems to hinge back and forth between—"

Rosalie opened her mouth to interrupt; I snapped, "What you gone do? Brood over the fact that people aren't who you need them to be? That Cowboy is a cop? Will always make cop choices? That China and Leonard went for the main chance—you. People will always go for the main chance."

"Life sucks."

"Who are you to demand that people go against their nature just because it would be more convenient for you if they were different?"

China couldn't stay quiet. "Leonard didn't get a chance to tell her what it's about because that fat pig-whorina came over and interrupted the goddamn visit."

Birdeye came in, sly, knowing. "Rosalie opened the pack already—whatever in there's long gone."

"Is not!"

"Gimme 'em. I bet they ain't nothin'."

"No." Rosalie put the cigarettes on the corner of my desk. Aligned the edges. We could see that the pack had been opened, sloppily folded back together.

China ambled over to Rosalie, grabbed her by the hair, pulled her head right back, pushed her own face near enough to kiss. "Listen to me, you slut. Listen real good."

Lily, never one to miss a chance, slid over then, snagged the pack, no one noticed.

"You hand me that pack nice as you can be."

Rosalie reached her hand around to where she'd left them, sputtering, "You give that man to me as a sweetheart on a platter, he tries to set me up, you pull my head off."

"Get real, girl. We work together here, now gimme that pack."

Frantic, Rosalie looked around for the pack.

Lily held the pack up, grinning. "These are no good. These here squares."

Rosalie reached a tentative hand out.

"Not so fast. You know what else was in here, don't you? What will you do for me if I give it to you?"

Rosalie stuck her lower lip out. Narrowed her eyes,

looked determined; I hoped she didn't realize that Lily could take her with one hand tied, I hoped she went for it, got the shit kicked out of her. I can't explain these sudden urges of mine, seem harmless enough.

But Birdeye walked over then, snatched the cigarettes out of Lily's hand. Expecting no resistance. Getting none. "Bow out, dog breath."

"I was only teasing, Birdeye. I wouldn't have given them your squares, honest." Lily edged toward the door.

China nodded to her in a forgiving way, her clever hands ripping into the pack. "Wow. I didn't know he was going to pull that old trick on Rosalie, passing her shit that way, I mean. I don't know what Johnson's trip was, really, Morgan, I'm sure it wasn't a setup."

Rosalie whined, "Well I don't know what else to call it."

"Nahhh. I mean! He just so fucking arrogant." Slitting the cigarettes with her long sharp fingernails, China oozed good humor, "Sucker nearly got us all busted, but it's okay now."

China pulled out a check. "Oh shit. Oh shit. Oh shit." She was not having a good day.

"What? Whatwhat what?" All of us. Lily came back in from the hall.

"The bloody asshole filled in his own fucking name!" China raised her eyes to the ceiling, held the check out like a three-day-old fish. "Here, lookit this! The bastard ruined it!"

Birdeye came over, picked it up, shrugging. "Well, we aren't any worse off than we were before."

"How you figure we not?" China's voice shook as she spoke, "Where the hell did he get these? No one except Roland, and he dead, knew where these were. How the hell Leonard get them?"

Rosalie, in a small voice, "Said they were behind a mirror in Varney's apartment."

China stopped cold. Then, "Bastard lie like a rug."

I could tell something about it hit her. "Come on. What's the deal?"

"Aw, nothin'. Nothin'. Look, these have to be signed by Rita Corazon—that's me. But how he expect me to sign these? Give the money to him?"

Birdeye said with a touch of incredulity, "Rita Corazon?"

"Never mind."

"Rita Corazon? That's your name?"

"Oh, Birdeye, never mind."

"Why he find 'em at Varney's?"

"Why he send 'em in with Rosalie?"

"What you askin' me for?" China shooed us away from the checks as if we were a flock of chickens. "Aw, listen, he don't know how to do checks right. He can't sign them or anything. That's my job. But he never should have involved Rosalie. Put him own funky goddamn name on there." She sort of gulped, "I don't know why he said he got them from Varney. He just crazed for coke. And pussy. You musta not given him any sugar, huh Rosalie? No wonder the man pissed off."

"What?"

"Generally he easy enough to push around. You know, the captive tongue." With some pride, "That's why he always need me."

"Pussy?"

"No. No. Nononono. He got a record as long as his dick, can't do stuff on his own. Rosalie was just supposed to keep an eye on him. Like she know from banks, can find out what he's up to."

"You wish."

"I suppose Leonard thinks he'll get these back all ready to cash."

"He didn't have time to say." Rosalie wasn't buying it.

"Well he sure as hell ain't." Musing, "Right after it happened, Roland's murder, you know, he got real strange." Her mind was working so fast I could hardly see her think, idea jumping on idea at such a rate that the early ones got lost. But somewhere in there was a thread that China didn't want me to pick up on.

Birdeye took Lily by the arm, pulled her out of the room.

China resumed, "I used to think Leonard killed him. You know, for the exercise. But he not that kind of man." She rearranged herself, smooth, like satin. "Now, Varney, on the other hand, she say she dancin' all night at some club. Same as I was at the bar. But I know she seen Roland that night. Dead." Nodding her head with old wisdom. "It's a shock to see someone with their head blown off even if you're ready for it. The way she was, after—she musta seen him."

"How you so sure?"

"Well," she paused.

I knew that rhythm. Lie like a rug.

Rosalie spoke up like the snotty girl in grade school who knew all the answers. Lied anyway. "Leonard told me he found Varney standing over Roland with the shotgun in her hand."

"Sound like he diddling the truth again. What he doin' there?"

"I guess he can stop in to see his own brother—"

"Come on, China."

"I don't know why he was there. Wondered about it myself—" Defiant. "To get some money. I guess. But it was long gone."

"How you know?"

"Oh. I just know these things."

A disaster. That real estate office was like a bus station, everyone who wanted to kill old Roland, for whatever reasons of their own, stopped by. Any one of half a dozen people could have got the money. If there was any money. Hell, maybe one of them offed him because there wasn't any money. I could see that. "Hey. You've got fourteen people swearing in depositions that you never left the bar. They lied?"

"Yeah. Of course, man. Anyone who wasn't on the hot sheet signed for me. I just stopped by for a minute anyway. To see. You know. To make sure I wasn't cut out of anything good." She smiled. "But everyone long gone when I got there."

We had little else to do but tell tell tell convoluted contrived unbelievable stories, build up the mythology. Need simple facts? Gone beyond recall.

"People think they slick, somebody swell, think maybe they have everybody on a string. Ha." China gave it awhile, just rolling the idea around her mouth, letting us suck on it too. She glanced at me. I scowled at her, she turned to Birdeye.

Birdeye spoke, undistracted, she had her own ideas about who killed Leonard. As did I. "None of this does us any good. How we gone cash these without Leonard?"

"Where'd Leonard really get them?"

"Aw, I dunno."

Rosalie spoke, prissy, "He said he got them in Varney's apartment."

China shrugged, made a face. "Shouldn't be believin' people so easy." Slow malice. "Roland didn't look like him, you know? He didn't look like nothing. Not nothing at all. It was hard to make the connection to Roland."

Just for a lark I asked, "How tall was Roland?"

China replied, puzzled, sincere. "About five foot nine maybe."

It didn't seem the appropriate time to mention that Leonard was listed as five foot nine and squeaky clean on her visiting list but showed up in person as a skinny crack freak somewhere around six feet tall. The man hadn't grown in the last years either now.

Fingerprints might not even explain who was who was who.

Fucking petty criminals.

Just one more reason why I work alone. Something clean about a well-executed burglary.

"How often you see Leonard on the streets?"

"Oh, hey, he was always disappearing, you know. He like, comes and goes."

"How often?"

Still trying to please me. "Every couple months maybe, he drift on by. Borrow some bread. Go off again."

"Not a bus driver?" Rosalie couldn't keep out of it.

China flipped her hand. "Oh well, that. Yeah, he was. Sometimes."

"But he's always been pretty much the same guy since you've known him?"

"Well sure? Who else he be?"

If that corpse was the original Leonard, and it was Roland visiting her as Leonard, China was the coolest broad in the place.

"Yeah? How did you know it was Roland if his head was blown off?"

"Oh no question, it was him. I'da known the rest of him in a headless lineup."

Rosalie, battered and confused, resented the whole thing. There didn't seem to be any simple murder, the way it should be: bang, the guy's gone. Curtains. End of story, everyone gets on with their lives who's still got them. No one gave a sweet shit about her problems, not least of which was getting busted in front of Cowboy, again. She should maybe get away from the company she was keeping. Call in sick until her interview with Cowboy. Beg the man to take her back. Blow job? What?

She leaned over China's shoulder. Irritated. She was the bank expert but no one was giving her credit. "Hell. Just countersign the damn things on the back with Leonard's signature, autograph them with your Rita Corazon business, I'll take 'em up front, cash 'em. No big thang." Cool. She felt so cool.

"Cash them? Where? At the officer's canteen?"

"Nahhh. It'll be a piece of cake." She spoke with false confidence. "We can work it out."

"We? We?" China shook her head, distant. "We?"

• SEVENTEEN •

I handed Birdeye a strip of tape, she patched the leak in the hose. "Is it going sour? What you think?"

Raisins. Honey. Yeast. Esoterica. Temperature controls. More complicated than tropical fish or bogus checks.

Birdeye tasted, judicious. "Another six hours at the most."

"For those two? Or the brew?"

"The brew. Those two be at each other's throats long before that. See what the idea of a little money can do."

Rosalie sat in my chair, smoking my cigarettes, enjoying that familiar money fever. Itchy palms. She thought there should be at least ten grand easy. She eyed China. There could be a great deal more.

I thought the whole thing had the stink of a straight-up con. I poured Birdeye and myself drinks, the other two didn't even notice.

China was buried in her own machinations, emotions flitting across her face like firefly enchantment, decisions and revisions that another day would shake. "Damn this prison anyway, makes a girl a living fool. Here's a ticket to the free world, pass Go, collect two hundred dollars. And I can't think straight."

Rosalie plotted what she'd do if she could get back into Cowboy's office, use the embossing machine up front: Make up a payroll, put another name on the logo, she could make those checks payable to God Almighty.

Might as well make them to God anyway, it looked like he was the only one who could cash them. Check out the Pope's action.

"Can't you just see Leonard trying to convince some steel-eye teller that she was supposed to give him a couple thou?"

China spoke again, "I can do them." Careful voice.

"Not just Rita Corazon. Leonard." A breath. "I can do just about anyone's signature." Delicate frown, warning Rosalie. "I'm an artist."

Birdeye came up out of her booze contemplation. "Can't you just see Leonard handing penny one of the money over to anyone if he got his hands on it?"

"It's got to be set up so the bag man is righteous."

"Dreamer."

Rosalie: "I can make those checks sail through—fifteen minutes with the machines up front. If only I was still in Cowboy's office."

China interrupted, "Wait a minute, you said how you can withdraw money from an ATM machine—transfer stuff over the phone—what we need is an ATM number."

"ATM. Right." Birdeye finished putting a plastic gang valve on the piece of hose in her hand. Muttering to me, "These two are going to buy out the Bank of America next week."

China grinned. "Okay, smart-ass. What do you suggest?"

"It be easy to get Rosalie back up front in her old job."

Rosalie looked alert. "What? An act of Congress?"

"Nah. I'll fix it so Cowboy's new secretary is too sick to work. You go up to fill in."

Rosalie waited for the other shoe to drop.

Birdeye put her head back down, paying attention to the important work at hand. She twisted a piece of wire around the hose. "Oh yeah. How many days you need?"

"How you gonna do this now?"

Birdeye looked at her as if she was really dumb. "Put some stuff in her clothes when I do them. Give her a rash. How long you need?"

"A rash? A rash? That's going to keep her away?"

Birdeye reattached the hose, put it back behind the books, leaned over to her. "Nothin' so awful as a itchy clit now, is there?"

Rosalie pulled back. "Oh. Could you make the rash permanent?"

These large innocent looking criminals are vicious.

"Hey now. That's taking things another step, hey? What you want to disable the girl for?"

"Oh never mind."

I thought I'd left them to their delirium long enough. In my most delicate voice: "Who is going to handle things on the street?"

They all looked at me, hope flickering and dying in their faces.

"Is there anyone, anyone at all we know who could be trusted to handle any amount of cash?"

"Well sure!"

"Yeah sure!"

"Who?"

"Rosalie's mamma?"

"Yo mamma. She won't do that. Want to know where it came from, where it going, and she won't believe it's all for charity. No, man, that's more trouble than it's worth. Believe me."

"Claudia?"

"She's so twisted up with her hormones she hardly has time to do her job in here."

"A little money on the side, set herself up independent?"

"Get real, girl."

China said in a defiant but insecure voice, "Oh never mind. It's my problem. I'll work it out."

"It's our problem too, girl."

Living on the edge. Inside a fading dream. The importance of everything becomes extreme, the near focus tightens, perfected. Everyone catches a part of the desperate energy. Sucks on it. Lives for it. Any moment you're going to get evicted, but in the meantime keep that pipe full. Live for today because tomorrow you're dead meat.

We'd all keep working on it.

■   ■   ■

After they left I smoked the few cigarettes Rosalie missed. Watched my smoke rings get blurry, fade into the general haze. Petty bullshit, unnecessary confusion. The rule of the law: Use scraps, leftovers, left-behinds, the fragments of other people's lives and ideas. Half those, fantasies. Nothing of any importance. What have we learned from this, what have we gained for all our trouble and pain?

I didn't give a flying fuck if the guy in the visiting room was Leonard or Roland or Tony the Loser, alive or dead, China's husband lover brother pimp. More: I didn't care if the bloody world came to an end. We'd still be locked up one on top of the other in some limbo warehouse with too many women, dramas, broken promises, empty lives; we'd all be back we'd all be back we'd watch each other get old fat unlovely we'd come and go and come again never quite making it standing in line the big break any day after day waiting.

Hey. It's no different on the streets. Same old same old. No reason to pretend that life out there is any better—by the time we get there ain't gone be any more goddamn room out there, end up shacking with some creep in a shooting gallery, hit the bricks wondering what to do where to go how to get over.

You can't get there from here.

Staring at the walls, filling the air with smoke.

Alexander stopped by, wearing his lawyer silk suit. Ooooh, looking good. We did a queer sort of dance—I held out my hand for a handshake, he grabbed it, pulled me to him, his other arm sliding around my shoulders.

I had already begun to like that. So much for the power of native intelligence when it's up against hormones.

"I missed him today, but there'll be another time—"

"Oh. That's okay, Alexander. I heard about it. Anyway I wouldn't want you to do something that could get you into trouble." This was hardly true but he didn't need to know that.

He stepped away. "Don't fucking patronize me, Morgan. I'm not a kid."

I considered contradicting him, decided against it. All this effort wasn't worth it. Nothing was.

We were alone in the small quarters of the library. I traced the fine lines of his profile in my mind as if there might be salvation in it.

Alexander fussed, "No one said a damn thing I understood up front except that Rosalie was fine. I figured she was fine. Why should she be anything but fine? Relatively speaking that is. What happened anyway?"

I waved my hand. "Oh nothing, one of those jailhouse misunderstandings. It's a good thing you didn't jam Leonard up. He might have dismembered you." I snickered in spite of myself. "Hey, Alexander, sit down." I lit two of his cigarettes, passed him the second. "You didn't come back here just to tell me you missed your connection with Leonard."

"Right." He smoothed his hair back with that movement I found so irritating, so attractive. "I found out someone is trying to reopen China's case, set China up as the perpetrator.

"She's never been tried for the actual murder, you know, she copped a plea on the solicitation, so double jeopardy protection doesn't apply." Succinct. Direct. On target.

The charm of the new day continued to falter.

He seemed to take pleasure in disturbing news. "China will at the very least be called upon to testify. If she is unwilling," I nodded that seemed likely, "she'll be subpoenaed as an unfriendly." I kept my mouth shut. "There might be something in it for her but it is hard to see what."

Hell, on the way to the hearing she could ask the escort to stop by a bank. Sounded good to me.

He continued, "The good news is that I got Roland's stats from the obits: exactly the same as the ones on the Leonard sheet up front."

"So?"

"Suppose Leonard's a contract killer!"

"Leonard?" These men made my brains hurt. "Can't you stop making a romance out of this?"

Reaching for a piece of paper, scribbling, Alexander ignored my plea. "See, Morgan, it's all so clear: Change the 'R' to 'Le.' Leave the 'o,' get rid of the top of the 'l' make it an 'n,' leave the 'a'—"

"So what?"

"The man changed his name! He really did! Or rather he changed his brother's name. Got himself clean statistics just so easyyyy. Seems to me that Leonard realized his time on the streets was gonna be short, so he got hold of Roland's ID, registered his own face with Roland's numbers for everything; you know, counting on the all black men look alike thing. He must've used it even before he killed him."

"What you mean, he killed him?"

"Well," he said, amateur hour for courtroom theatrics, "it might seem a pretty dumb move for Leonard to kill Roland for the statistics. Unless!" He paused. More drama.

I hoped someone straightened him out on his presentation before he took on an important case.

"See, Roland didn't want to share his vital stats with his outlaw brother. That could," Alexander pondered out loud, "lead to some serious disagreements."

He leaned forward, confident. "Leonard is the one. Just feels right. It's weird. But there it is."

Asshole couldn't even do a check right. Not a murderer. Gigolo was more like it. Gigolo. Nice old-fashioned simple word. "How'd you find out about them reopening China's case anyway?"

"I said I was China's attorney."

"Ooh. That's good. Shall we tell her?"

"Come on, Morgan."

"What have you gotten on Varney?"

"Who?"

"The mysterious redhead."

"Redhead? Not a mention."

"Find her. Fast. She's a major player. She was there that night."

"How you know this?"

"China said so."

"Why the hell didn't you tell me?"

"I just did. It may be true. Or not. People aren't always truthful, you know. A lot of the time it doesn't matter."

"Do they do this just to consternate us?"

Us? Us? How sweet. "China says whoever killed him got away with a lot of money."

"How she know? She there?"

"Ah, there you're stepping into the area of attorney-client confidentiality."

Severe. "I'm the attorney."

"Then ask your client. Shit, Alexander, you've got to find out what's going on."

"What's in it for me?" He was bluffing. By this time he would have crawled through a quarter mile of broken glass just to get a whiff of my shorts—he liked the rush, the women, the plots, the secret silent relentless sexuality.

I set one up for each of us. He grinned crookedly. "I was a little slow getting up the next day. Perhaps I should restrict myself to only one."

"Sleep in then. Life's a bitch, then you die."

Alexander was, after all, China's attorney. Even if China didn't know it yet. She'd be needing one if things continued as they were. And as her attorney it would be a typical, accepted procedure for him to handle some of her business affairs. Checks. Discreetly.

I poured us each a stiff one.

"I can't keep leaving here shit-faced, Morgan. One of these days someone will snap."

"Cheers. Deny everything, darling."

• EIGHTEEN •

China stopped by later that afternoon; she'd been thinking, she said, that maybe Alexander could handle the little detail of the checks for her.

While I'd been thinking along those lines myself it seemed a good idea. But if China thought so it had to be dead wrong. I may have been enchanted with her body, but that devious mind of hers froze me right in my tracks.

"Birdeye isn't going to like any of this."

She put her warm hand over mine, placed her cigarette between my lips. "We won't tell her then."

I felt a sinking sensation right below my rib cage.

■   ■   ■

Rosalie went to work back up front. Noble. Obliging. Accurate. Brave courageous kind. She wore perfume. Said it was good to be around a man.

Brought Cowboy coffee, fixed the way he liked it; she wasn't going to let him forget for one minute just what he might let slip out of his hands if he didn't take some aggressive steps with the classification committee. He seemed pleased.

She kept her eye on the room with the printer. Timing the access, watching the watchers. Ten minutes was all she'd need. Fifteen at the most. The checks were going to be works of art, designed to impress a select audience. Hell, China wasn't the only artist around there. It would go smooth as smooth, a check of hers had never yet failed, wasn't going to now, either.

Cowboy interrupted her reverie by handing her pages of the other woman's work to do over, put his hand on her shoulder while he explained how nice it was to have her back. She sifted through the work, appalled at the mistakes.

Blurted, "Were you getting laid or what?"

He didn't take his hand away, sort of hummed a question at her, not listening to what she asked.

"Hey. That girl isn't any kind of secretary, that's obvious." The hell with it. She might as well try for the whole enchilada. "I heard you don't want me back up here because you been fucking that girl."

Cowboy had turned away from her to sign the watch report, the back of his neck seemed to get a little more color to it, his voice sounded thick, surprised. "Say what?"

"Oh come on." She walked over to stand behind him.

"I don't have to screw around in here to get laid, Rosalie."

Turning around, his face was inches away from hers. "I have a diverse population out there to choose from. You now, you are in a far more limited position."

"Not a lot of women want to date a prison guard, man." She pouted at him. He took a long time answering.

"Could you do that again. With some feeling?"

He was always the gentleman. Happy to oblige. She liked the taste of him, chewed on his mustache, purring. She turned her face up asking for more, felt him tremble lightly. She would be out of the cafeteria for good by the end of the week.

■   ■   ■

After interminable dithering about his conscience and legal responsibilities, Alexander agreed to handle China's money. Started to track Varney down. Grumbled a lot to me while admitting he'd left himself open when he said he was China's lawyer in the first place.

Although he said he didn't talk with his father about it, he must have mentioned something, in the theoretical way he learned in law school; he didn't think his father heard him, the old man seemed to be just grunting to himself over brandy and cigars: "Always get your cut, son. Always get your cut."

That was perhaps not what Alexander needed to hear.

I repeated in a hypnotic drone how it was all entirely legal, the money to cover the check was in the account, there was nothing for him to be upset about. It was an honorable thing to do. He ignored the warning bells. So did I.

I gave him another drink.

He slumped over it, head down, elbows spread, mumbling to himself, "It's easy, huh. I set up a trust account or a business account or something for China, deposit these mystery checks China gets. It's her pension? Or what?"

"Well, yeah. You could call it a pension if you wanted to. What's so complicated?"

"It's spelled *fraud*, Morgan. Forgery. Bribery." He straightened up. "I have to get out of here, everything with you women gets insane."

He stood up. Put his glass down with a snap. "Accessory to murder."

"Don't get grandiose, Alexander."

I felt very self-confident. "You're making things more complicated than they are. Listen," I cooed, "the next thing you do is get her an ATM card, everything attached to the account, hook up other accounts to it—"

"You are kidding."

I poured him another glass, smiled deep into his eyes. He had pretty eyes, weird flecks in them, odd I hadn't noticed before.

■   ■   ■

Rosalie put the final touches on the check, a beautiful $17,185 version; she'd abstracted it from the pack before turning it over to China. Rita Corazon couldn't deposit that one, only Rosalie could. She thought of it as her fee. Girl has to protect her own interests.

She got an outside line on Cowboy's phone, dialed Leonard's number. By the time she hung up she was smiling, life was getting sweeter by the day, jail was no barrier to a stepper, just got to know how to do things right.

She was typing Alexander's name on the envelope for China's Rita Corazon check when the office erupted into chaos around her.

Her natural first reaction was that she herself was the center of attention. Essential paranoia. Not entirely inappropriate. Not, however, necessary in this case.

She might have more fully appreciated the panic if it had not been outstripped by her own.

She hardly had time to put China's check in Alexander's envelope before Cowboy cornered her, pulling his curly hair out.

"You look distraught." Wifely concern seemed best.

"No shit. There's a frozen count. Someone's escaped."

He stopped, searching for the words. Embarrassed. "They stole the fucking perimeter truck."

"How'd they do that?"

"The perimeter guard pulled into the front lot." He struggled. "The idiot dashed inside to take a piss—"

Rosalie could hardly keep a straight face. Oh the horror the horror. Next best thing to a general pardon. She kissed Cowboy on the cheek. "Poor dear."

She slipped China's check into Alexander's box on her way out.

■　　■　　■

They called the state police.

Rumors rippled up the hallways in waves of speculation. Forty-five minutes into it thin voices could be heard screaming from one unit to the next. It was Lily. Free at last. Free at last.

Details began to pile up as women returned from their occupations in outlying corners of the prison.

"Lily climb up that big old tree, leap about twelve feet onto the roof of the visiting room, lay there flat as a cow pie just watching what turn up. That big German perimeter guard drive up in the truck, dash in the front gate to take a piss. Quick as shit Lily dive into the parking lot. Crazy fucker stole the perimeter truck. Shotgun strapped to the dash."

"She already made it out of the state."

The administration took it all quite seriously. Vicious convict escapes! Attacks guard. Steals truck. Guns! Disappears! The whole of Western civilization is on the brink. Looook out.

Claudia's jaw pushed forward as she walked up the halls counting bodies like some frigging warehouseman. Frozen count. Half the silly bitches were screwing around somewhere, they certainly weren't in their cells. Madness. Chaos.

"Where the hell have you been?"

"Everyone in the school building had to be counted there before coming back here to be counted again. Why you so upset?"

"I'm not upset. I'm not upset. Just get in that cell."

"Hey. Whatever it is, keep it to yourself, huh?" I pushed the side of my face up to the wicket hole. "Like it's a crime to want out of here?"

Claudia didn't know what the problem was with everyone, even the good ones were mouthing off. She didn't deserve this. Bunch of good for nothing whores anyway. Claudia sighed. She didn't suppose that was the right attitude either. Why in hell that mindless freak escaped . . .

Everything that could go wrong did go wrong. Her period was late. The phone in Control was ringing. The last two women she counted were pretending to hang themselves with invisible rope.

"Claudia here, in the process of count."

Pause for masculine squeaking over the line. Then Claudia: "No shit? I mean, oh that's too bad, sir. Yes, sir."

The truck had been spotted, no Lily, no shotgun. She was told to keep a steady eye on us. The guards had to check every corner of the prison, count every body twice. It was procedure. We hollered for our lunch. But the guards followed procedure: Lily could be just the frontrunner in a cleverly planned mass breakout.

No one was pleased with a frozen count at lunch. The police of course liked it just fine when we were locked down, less trouble all around, they knew where we all were, could catch up on some of the paperwork. But not at lunch. Lunch was one of those things that just had to be taken care of.

The phone lines were electric between the units: Of course the women should be let out to eat. Nobody wanted to bag up a thousand damn lunches. Response from the administration: Of course the women should be left locked down, it was procedure after an escape. They might all rush the fence, without convicts they'd have no jobs. Come on, be reasonable.

The guards in the units bitched. The big cheeses wouldn't have to bag and deliver all those lunches. Oh no, not *them*. They were busy giving press statements. There's just some things that can't be explained. So why don't those fat cats come on down into the rest of the prison, start bagging up lunches.

Our captive voices clamored anew.

Claudia bellowed, "Okay, ladies. Shut up." We did so. "It's still a frozen count, ladies. I want you in your cells sitting upright on your beds. I must be able to see a living breathing body. No headstands. This is serious here."

Screams of glee.

"Oh just shut up, would you." Claudia felt sorry for herself as she plodded up the hall. No sign of Lily. The woman had disappeared. Stone gone. They found the truck. No gun.

Typical, Claudia thought, just typical.

"Ya-zoo! Newsflash here now, ladies: Miss Lily has gone for the gold. She holdin' uppa bank in Century City right now—"

Claudia thought her head was going to crack. "Shut up shut up. All of you."

It was going to be the straight and narrow for her. No more fucking around. Please, God, just make these bitches shut up, have my period come, have my husband disappear, probably it be best if you returned Lily. Simplify everything. It's going to be hell in here if she manages to stay out. Listen to me now, God, it will be hell.

Lily had made it. No one begrudged her that. Well done too. The lock-down continued for an hour. Another one. Another. We hollered ourselves hoarse, stared at our toes or navels, finally came around to blaming Lily for every inconvenience, smoked up all our cigarettes.

Claudia was fuming, the place was a psycho ward. Between the damn phone and the bitches demanding painkillers there were other pranks: Queenie put her towel out the wicket, asked Claudia to deliver a pack of cigarettes to Narcisse and me. We were, she'd heard correctly, all out.

"I'm not the goddamn postman."

"Torture is illegal now, Claudia. You don't want no one goin' off locked up in here, you know what it leads to. Murder, mayhem, antisocial behavior."

"Fuck you." Claudia was not pleased. Came back in five minutes. Might as well. It was no more petty than anything else she was supposed to be doing. "Oh hell. Gimme 'em."

When we were let out to eat, first the trusties, then the kitchen workers, one side of a unit at a time; there was a solemn triumphant gleam in everyone's eyes.

"After you bus your dishes, ladies, return directly to your cottages, there will be another count taken. There will be another count taken. Return directly to your cottages. Go back and lock in your cells, ladies."

"Good thing I put that check in Alexander's box, huh?" Rosalie made it a point to mention it.

"I don't know, Rosalie. I have a bad feeling."

"Ladies! Ladies! All privileges have been canceled until further notice. You will return to your cottages and lock in after you bus your dishes. No exceptions."

"What? Can they do that?"

No classes. No night activities. No visits, no packages, no commissary.

Therefore no cigarettes.

No question: Cigarettes are in the Prisoner's Bill of Rights. Right up there with food to eat, air to breathe. The due process right comes and goes, but cigarettes are stone guaranteed. It's in the Constitution. Read the small print.

Contrary to what they say, that doesn't make life in prison a bed of cherries. (Bowl of roses?) Even a couple cartons of Shermans or Balkan Sobranies is a great, great thing, but it's not the fullness and goodness of life.

"What they think, we join up forces with Lily, put the place to the torch, huh?"

"Lily gone lookin' for that slick fucker she tried to kill once already—"

"Nah, she driving down the coast in a red Camaro, smokin' a big spliff—"

The world was cut off except for television, radio. No one had more than three or four packs of cigarettes. People got to feeling strange. A little closer to the edge than usual.

• NINETEEN •

Alexander tried to get inside, he cajoled the woman working the front desk: He had unfinished business in the classroom. Had to pick up some stuff in the old school building. He needed. He expected. He was privileged. No way. He was pissed.

Narcisse, making a burger delivery to the officers at the front desk, watched him check his box to see if any papers had been turned in for him, saw him pick up some papers, envelopes. He opened one as he walked toward his car. It looked like a paycheck to Narcisse.

She saw Leonard get out of a taxicab at the front gate, hurry inside where he was short-stopped just like Alexander. Unsuccessful in his negotiations with the officer at the front desk, he retreated into the parking lot looking displeased. Alexander leaned on the fender of his car, smoking. Leonard strolled over to him.

Narcisse was escorted back to our cell.

■   ■   ■

Two days later telephone privileges were reinstated on an emergency basis. I decided I had to make a call for Narcisse the Silent. Claudia thought that sounded plausible, she wasn't too interested, having those problems of her own and all. Waved me to the extension phone, dialed the number I gave her.

She was conducting some private personal research with China. She thought her exotic bartender might be Mexican, she came straight to the point: "How are Mexican men as husbands?"

"Oh, Claudia! What is this now?" Coy. "It's true that they are gorgeous. But a Latino man isn't always easy to have around the house—"

My voice came over the office phone speaker, "Collect call for Alexander, from Morgan, will you accept the charges?"

"Sure."

We made the usual opening remarks, how funny our voices sounded, how nice it was to talk, etc. Formal, casual, esoteric information hidden in every phrase; I wanted to make sure he got the check that was in his box, but before I could get to that he told me some news of his own.

"I gave our mutual friend a ride home today, an educational little trip. He'd been trying to get in to see Rosalie, she'd asked him to come—kiss and make up, huh?"

"Huh? He was here to see who?"

"Yeah. Rosalie. Seemed to have been important. Oh well. I got Varney's phone number out of him, give her a call later tonight, sell her some life insurance. Slick work, huh?"

"Uh." My mind was spaghetti. "Uh. You check your box?"

"Yeah. Term papers. Why? You sending me love letters at last?"

"You mean you didn't get it?"

"What? Oooh, Morgan. A love letter to me?"

"Huh? No way." I could see into the office where our conversation was coming over the Control tap. His attitude, tone of voice, everything bothered me. "Alexander. Are you sure about this?"

"Sure about what, sweetheart?"

"Leonard came to see Rosalie? And nothing in your box?"

"Yeah. He said she called him, it was urgent. So what?"

I could see China sit up like she'd been goosed.

"And you didn't get my, ah, letter?"

"No, honey, but I'll come right over now—"

China bolted from the office leaving Claudia to mutter, "What the hell?"

As I raced past the office I heard Alexander's phone-thin voice hollering, "Hey! Hey! Anyone there?"

Claudia's mouth fell open with confusion. Mostly, cop responses aside, I think she felt left out.

I found China holding Rosalie by the throat, pushing the big girl's face up against the wall. "I'm going to cut your face off, make you eat it you don't give me that check. Get it for me. Now."

Since China had her by the throat it was impossible for Rosalie to say anything, but she tried.

"Wait a minute here." My voice, due to shock, had an authoritative crack. I wished I could cultivate that.

China eased up. "I kill people who rip me off."

I looked without much sympathy at Rosalie shivering and rubbing her throat. "What'd you do with the check?"

Croaking, "I put it in Alexander's box."

I didn't believe her. "You put it in his box? Which one?"

"Ah." Rosalie thought. "The one up front."

China went for her again, I dragged China off.

"Just keep an eye on her while I go through her shit. If it's here, we'll find it." I half-buried myself in the closet to feel behind Rosalie's television set. I figured I could find it in fifteen minutes. If it was here. My hands were sweating.

Behind my back China must have gone at her again, I could hear one of them shrieking.

Claudia tiptoed up to the cell. "Well, ladies. You mind explaining?"

"Huh? Rosalie don't feel so good—wanna get her an aspirin or something?"

"I don't intend to get anything for you until you tell me what's going on."

I could see Rosalie wanted to play it both ways but China's hand was clawed into her back like a blade.

"Oh, Claudia. Get off it. We just had an idea, like ESP, you know. Came down here to find Rosie's got a sore throat or something."

Two junkies up the hall, bless their larcenous hearts, got into a screaming fight over nothing, Claudia had to

leave us. She made each of us go lock in our own cells. No
showers. No mayhem.

I whispered, "Hey, China, you can stop payment on it if
it's gone missing."

"I'm gone kill that girl."

I don't know what I thought about killing, seemed that
Alexander might deserve a little killing. I couldn't believe
he'd be so flip if he'd gotten it. Maybe Narcisse could
check his box tomorrow if she got a chance. If we got
unlocked.

• TWENTY •

Birdeye, like other edge dwellers, did not appreciate additional restriction. She didn't have that much more time to do, planned on spending most of it on China's cot, but it seemed to her that China had other things on her mind. Money.

Birdeye was sick of the whole thing, China wouldn't leave it alone.

Rosalie kept pleading, "Hell, China, almost anything could have happened to that check, you know? Cowboy just walked right in on me. Fucking Lily—screwing everything up."

Rosalie got a handful of tranks from the clinic and locked herself in her cell.

China gave her two days to come up with either the check or the cash.

Birdeye stopped talking to China. International incident.

China shut everyone out, did junk. Offered to do some tattoo work for me. I passed on it.

"Just a little design, you know, it'd look nice."

I told her she was out of her mind.

"Damn. If I was just out, just out for a week, a day. I'd straighten everything out." She spoke from a nod. "Hit a couple dozen damn banks, one day, then I'd come back, Morgan, do this time without a care in the world. Just one day outside." She tapped my hooch cup with her long red fingernail, I filled the cup, handed it to her, she drained it. "I figure I ain't gone get it though. Damn." China frowned at her sketch: a lady saint holding a bloody sword.

"Who's the victim?"

"Me. You. Ever'body. Shit."

We went outside to catch a breath of air, the law business

was slow. I hadn't heard from Alexander.

Birdeye had reached some kind of critical mass. Fucking prison. China. Checks. Christmas. She had been looking forward to fucking her way through Christmas up to her early January parole. Didn't look like it was gone happen.

She grabbed the lopsided Christmas tree, dragged it out of the rec room, corny paper ornaments falling in its wake; the cold winter daylight made the scrubby little tree look forlorn as Birdeye walked around it, intoning solemn ritual curses.

We wandered over, filled with the general malaise.

"Isn't right, this."

"What you expect? This is prison, girl."

"For reals."

"They gone kill her, they find her."

"I'm gone kill 'er I find 'er. Fuck up my Christmas."

"Ain't gone find 'er. Lily long gone from around here."

"Said on the news an old guy held up a liquor store in town. Was probably her."

"No way. She gone."

"The news. Jeez. Hey, did you hear the press release about it? She armed and dangerous. Armed and dangerous."

"That some consolation."

Birdeye flicked her lighter once or twice, then leaned forward to watch the tree catch on fire. It burned with a satisfying snap.

Thea, who'd never learned to fear fire or anything else, grabbed its stubby trunk, flipped it end over end in a great flaming arc toward the center of the circle. Perversely, it went out. Perverse, we trotted over, started it up again.

The little burning tree gathered quite a crowd. Hasty loudspeaker voices. We murmured among ourselves, casual, discussing the bonfire. There wasn't any plan or purpose behind the thing, it was spontaneous. Spon-taneous.

There was something proud, heady, about everybody

ignoring the voice of authority. It didn't happen often in prison. We watched women spinning in circles with their arms wrapped around each other, tossing Christmas ornaments like colored footballs, hoping simply to prolong the rush.

"*Ladies! La-dies!!* Return to your cottages!!"

We stood our ground, grinning. More trees were dragged over, surprised guards chasing along behind, raving about the Christmas spirit. Tra-dition.

A few garbage cans made a noisy rolling ambush as the guards turned the corner, more got thrown at the windows. Fires leaped up, expanded like Chinese fireworks.

"Anyone not in their cells in five minutes will be in *deeep trouble!*"

It all was very satisfactory.

Thea and Queenie had jimmied a side window in the clinic, were methodically stowing anything that even looked like it might fly, when, much to their dismay, ravening banshee women crashed in the front door.

Birdeye went through the main guard's desk, looking for the keys to the dispensary. "Where the hell is Morgan? This be a piece of cake for her. Hey—somebody go find Morgan."

I had business of my own, elsewhere.

No one was certain where the guards were, they seemed to have scattered like a flock of little birds when the mob came crashing in the door. Wise move. Convenient anyway.

China went down the hall to the lab, a supply of clean points would make life infinitely easier, all anyone else was coming up with were Band-Aids, aspirin. Someone suggested that that's all they used even for surgery. Thea slammed the door off another locked cabinet. Nothing.

"Never any medicine when you want it in here anyway. Might as well go back outside." Thea flashed a self-satisfied smile which belied her words. Her pockets were bulging with material for sales, concoctions.

Queenie came out of surgery looking righteously

pissed. "No painkillers anywhere except for Tylenol, fucking Vicoden."

"Grab the Vicoden—it's not bad by the handful, girl!"

"Grab it yourself, this place is history."

When Queenie looked questions at Thea she nodded
with the tiniest of smiles. Scored again, dearies. Scored
again.

Rubbish was pushed up against the buildings, set on
fire. Women stood around hopping from one foot to the
other waiting for the walls to come tumbling down. The
place was all bricks and concrete so it didn't happen.
Most of us thought about hitting the fence, then decided
to party awhile, go back to our cells, lock in. Prepare for
another day.

The voice from the loudspeaker seemed to make every
announcement over and over again. In Swahili for all the
attention it got.

Hup hup hup the guards from the men's prison came
in, lined up with their shiny white helmets glowing by the
light of the perimeter spots like hundreds of eggs. They
trotted around in little circles of a dozen men apiece looking grim. Ten-shun. Face masks in place. Batons at the
ready. Shotguns. Tear-gas canisters. Ready ready ready.

The men lumbered forward in step, batons horizontal,
shields forming a solid reflecting wall. As the tactical
squad went through its proto-military rituals the women
closest to them took up positions in the shadows, no
special plans, simple curiosity.

The men formed up again. Trotting in place.

The tactical squads were annoyed, nothing more, at
the crazy women banshee-hooting, tossing burned trees
and garbage in the air. It seemed a messy but cheerful sort
of riot.

But these special squads were unfamiliar with the lay-
out of the place. Strangers to the terrain, the shortcuts. It
seemed a simple matter, since the place was so flat, to go
in, subdue us with masculinity and tear gas, accept the
grateful thanks of the administration, buzz off for beers.

When their strategic maneuvers had little or no effect they fired off their tear gas in every direction, swearing manfully when the wind shifted. They used their clubs with a rhythmic whistling sound, smashed the little crowds of women. "Get back, damn you. Get out of the way!" The men realized that there was no place to put us, all the cell blocks filled with tear gas. They tried to bludgeon us into the ground.

There was a pause while the men formed up again, adjusting their gas masks, breathing heavily; Birdeye and China set up a wet towel brigade, an emergency medical station by the drinking fountain: witch hazel and Vaseline for tear-gas burns, Tylenol and Band-Aids for bruises. The best the clinic had to offer.

Most of us know enough to be able to do some fancy flying on adrenaline alone in situations like these.

Narcisse stood at the edge of the circle, looking confused. She came up out of her late afternoon nod feeling the weird energy on her arms, face, every part of her skin that was exposed to the air, a racing rippling effect that began to affect her stomach, then her eyes began to run and sting; as she emerged into the yard she stopped, puzzled. A party, a play, everything reversed. A carnival?

Deuce knew how to suck the best moments dry so they could be recycled. She danced up to Narcisse, a pirate scarf around her head, her eyes gleaming, she smeared Vaseline around Narcisse's eyes against the tear gas, gave her a bandana to cover her mouth, big gloves for her hands. They disappeared into the smoke together.

Birdeye saw them, still together, dodging easily through the police lines toward the security light poles. They strung clothesline rope knee-high in a web. A matter of a few seconds. Darted back into the swirling crowd; with their leather gloves they were able to pick up a couple spitting tear-gas canisters, toss them back at the helmets.

The advancing line of men broke with a gratifying stagger, retreated to fall tangled in the clothesline web.

Thea and Queenie turned the fire hose on them, main valve all the way open.

Rosalie, terrified, started to lock in her cell, realized she'd be murdered in there, dashed back outside. Flames tear gas screams delirium. Visions of massacres floated in her head.

China spotted Rosalie rushing up toward the administration building. China tackled her, pinning the larger woman to the ground. Birdeye, sighing, walked over, pulled China off. There were times and times for that.

Rosalie staggered away, saw Cowboy standing in the lobby of the administration building. He was wearing some fancy civilian clothes, grinding a cigarette out on the linoleum; on his way to a football game when he heard the emergency call on his truck's CB, he was wishing with every passing second that he'd gone on to the game. He didn't approve of the riot squad running amok any more than he liked his girls turning into witches and demons.

The warden still hadn't shown up. Typical. It looked like it was going to be his baby. Madness. He went into his office. Rosalie followed. She put herself trembling in his arms.

After awhile they started contacting the units, Rosalie automatically taking the messages down, marking locations on the prison floor plan. Here be monsters.

Cowboy's office door was torn open to frame Johnson, miserable, hair all frizzy, her uniform torn and dirty, she swayed, hysterical, demanding. She'd been killed, she said. She wanted medical attention *now.* "Now now nownownownow."

Rosalie didn't have time. "Get your ragged ass to the clinic then. We're busy."

Johnson wailed, "There's nobody there. I'm dying. No one cares."

Cowboy continued giving orders over the special com line in a concise even voice, ignoring the two of them.

Rosalie walked over, moved Johnson out of the office, shut the door on her.

"Well?" Cowboy looked up from the board, deep lines of tension on his face. "Get me the hospital. See if there's really no one there."

"Of course there is. She just came here because she thought you'd protect her."

Cowboy grunted in exasperation, "Like you."

She didn't answer him; lucky she'd gotten there first.

Birdeye rediscovered China sneaking around behind the police lines, moving toward the fence. "Let's get the hell out of here."

They stood nose to nose arguing. "Forget this shit. You never know what you're doing anyway."

Flames all around. Showed real dedication. Single-mindedness. If they'd put that much energy into their crimes they'd never have gotten caught.

Birdeye waved her arms at the scene around them. "You can't escape now, with no one to meet you. Streets are all blocked with this whole thing goin' on, everything all in a mess. First time you try for that money they gone pop you, girl. They gone get you on the full murder beef."

"Say what?"

"I know. Finally figured it out. You were steppin' out on your old man. With his own brother. That why you wanted to off him." Birdeye pushed her face right up in China's. "Can't kill someone then pretend you didn't. Either you killed Roland or you hired Leonard to do it. But you got the time, girl. What it is."

"You sick, Birdeye. You sick in the head. Now of all times. What is it with you anyway?"

The riot squad stopped tear-gassing themselves for the moment, began to regroup not fifteen feet away from where Birdeye and China argued in the smoke. Birdeye pulled China into the dirt, leaving the argument for another day, as rubber bullets sang just over their heads, thud into the wall behind them.

"I think I'm gone throw up."

"Just stay low. They don't even know we here."

They slithered off on their bellies toward the school building where I was doing some serious work.

I knew the procedure. If the convicts didn't trash the place, the police certainly would. I had to get the hooch out of the law library, or it could be the extinction of all sentient life on the planet.

Birdeye and China were almost on top of me before they noticed me crouched low in front of the last lock into the law library.

"Holy Mother of God. We haven't got enough time!"

I was glad for their help, it was complicated to dismantle the still in the half-light, the hoses were tangling, stinking liquid dribbled out on our clothes, on the floor, drooling on the books every time we looked away. We worried under our breath about where to hide the parts so it could be reassembled.

Thea and Queenie drove up in an electric golf cart the guards used to transport themselves from one end of the compound to the other, we piled the still in the back, cradling the bottles of finished hooch in towels. I rushed back in to do a cursory mop-up, pick up a couple files, relock the doors.

Wet towels over our faces, we raced through the surging crowds back to our deserted unit, peeled the heating vent cover off the wall in the rec room, plopped the still inside. The heating system hadn't worked in years.

The rest of the hooch hidden in our cells, we headed back outside just in time to see two cops moving up behind Narcisse with unnecessary stealth. Deuce screamed. Narcisse seemed to sense something, began to turn. One of the men grabbed her, the other slammed his club slicing against the back of her skull.

They didn't give her a glance as they moved forward to secure the next ten yards. Deuce heaved a brick at one of them, he fell to his knees.

Narcisse didn't quite lose consciousness, she was unaware of her blood slopping with raindrop sounds into the dirt. She tried to stand up, bringing her legs under her chest, bracing herself with her arms against the dizziness, the pain. Forcing herself upright, she held onto the building for support. Clouds of tear gas obscured the light, the eerie flickering of the little fires distorted people, elongated the shadows, the world askew, sloping at an unpleasant angle. She vomited.

Deuce reached her arms out, crooning; oblivious, Narcisse made small mewling sounds, touching her face and head with unbelieving hands. We carried her over to the water fountain, Deuce washed and wrapped her head, murmuring to her, forgetting perhaps that Narcisse couldn't hear, talking just to give herself the comfort of a voice.

The frantic loudspeaker still blared orders in a steady hysterical scream, water hoses squirted the riot squad from all directions, there was the eerie pop and hiss of tear gas, the sporadic thudding of rubber bullets. It was late.

Thea and Queenie hunkered at the base of a tree, swigging hooch, commenting on the show, a thin wire strung chin-high across the path. They were looking for a decapitation.

Birdeye and China jammed back to the cart. They drove through the lines of battle, screamed toward the farthest fence.

China noticed a portly figure wandering around, poking at the edges of the scrub.

"That's Old fucking Norah!"

"Yeaaaaaah! Let's get her."

The cart charged off the path, bouncing toward the old woman. Norah turned in the light-split night, her arms up in a warding gesture. The cart kept coming at her. She began to run, hop-trundling over the ruts, scampering toward some nonexistent shelter, her voice a high outraged whine.

She fell face first into the earth, they missed her by inches.

Jubilant, they drove the cart straight into the fence where it stopped, its electrical charge all used up.

"Grand theft auto. Again."

"That ain't gonna be all."

• TWENTY–ONE •

The day's first light was greeted by an animal groan. It had been an innocent, spontaneous eruption, not the result of grand decisions, delusions, coming to fruition in wild revelry and riot. It was just something that happened. Happens all the time, living on the edge. Sometimes it's a little bigger. Sometimes it's not such a good idea. Locked in our damp smoke-stinking cells, we thought it wasn't such a good idea.

But we might as well be proud of our little riot. We certainly weren't going to be comfortable.

The smell of the smoke and tear gas clung to our hair, our clothes, half the cells were still puddled with water from the fire hoses. We woke, still locked up after all, regretting that we didn't grab the opportunity to split when there was the chance.

We had crossed the line into anarchy only to find ourselves at the mercy of crazed, embarrassed police, satiated in an almost sexual way by the mutual frenzy that had taken place.

We figured we could be facing wholesale annihilation.

Narcisse lay on the bunk below me whimpering like a kitten, then she sat upright staring with a sad stricken look on her face. She did not respond to me.

"Please." I clutched my hands together, then grabbed my own head. "Please. Does your head still hurt?" I knew it did of course, but in sign language I depended on certain niceties, social necessities, no matter how inane.

Narcisse, with her years of practice, did not even have to try to ignore me.

A brown bag plopped on the floor with a squishy sound. Breakfast was an unbuttered slice of white bread, a badly cracked hard-boiled egg. The police must have been up half the night boiling eggs. Not much comfort.

China screamed out the wicket hole for coffee. The chant was taken up. Officer Johnson turned purple, ducked back into Control. She looked as if she hadn't slept for a week. Or fucked in a lifetime. One was true.

Deuce took a long pull on her bottle of hooch, lined up the tranks she'd gotten from Rosalie. Who woulda thought? Her first riot. For all the time she'd done, her very first. She hollered out her wicket hole, "Might as well all pass out for the next week, this the kind of chow they be givin' us."

Thea and Queenie sucked the sugar coating off some pills, melted them down, tied their arms off, banged them. Blood silver needle balancing up and down in and out around and down. They nodded in peaceful junkie sympathy, memories flooding their veins.

I paced the cell watching Narcisse for signs of I didn't know what. Coma?

Deuce's voice floated down the hall again, thick, content, "One Christmas when I was underage me and my girlfriends put together forty dollars, gave it to this old guy to buy liquor for us. He was somebody's uncle, stayed above the grocery, various old women stopped in and out, cleaning, cooking, taking care of him. He could forget things sometimes so it was good they checked in on him. He had a kind of cheerful gleam in his eyes, got right out warped, now and again."

We all settled back quiet to hear. I began to translate for Narcisse. Her eyes seemed to take on some focus.

"We hadn't been paranoid or anything, he wasn't going to rip us off since he lived right there in the neighborhood above the grocery. But then when the liquor store guy went around to the back room to get some of the bottles for our order, man, something just snapped in the old geezer's head. Like he went on automatic. He fucking grabbed up the whole damn cash register, came staggerin' out of the store hugging it, half falling down.

"Seize the time, you know. There he come, steady making progress down the street, slopping to the left side, then to the other, like the sidewalk was rolling. Nearly dropped the thing, caught it, straightening out at the last moment. We didn't know if we should applaud him or kill him.

"Of course we weren't entirely wrapped up in the spectacle right then. I mean, there went our forty fucking dollars, no booze.

"But to have seen it—to have been there."

Murmurs of assent from the adjoining cells.

"The wild-eyed liquor store guy just standin' on the sidewalk with his mouth open watchin' our old geezer make off with the cash register. He didn't even go for his gun or anything. You know, maybe it was worth it."

The ugly morning almost made me forget the pleasure of defiance, but in listening to Deuce's silly story I felt a very small smile growing.

Narcisse half grinned, asked me to make us tea, putting her hands to her head in unnecessary explanation. I'd never made her tea before, but following her severe directions I managed to make us two rather grainy cups of opium tea. We drank.

I lay back on the upper bunk signing to Narcisse that I hoped to hell I didn't roll out of bed when I passed out.

■   ■   ■

The administration got very busy while we slept, shipping out all the women they were housing for the feds, playing it down for the press; they claimed overcrowding as the prime reason for the riot. Pass a law, make people get up off more money, build more prisons.

A special session judge told them to give out earlier dates to shrink the population: Birdeye got one of the golden slips. "Ooo-ooh. Looky here looky here looky here."

Birdeye was already packed up. Just hoping to get gone before someone remembered to tell the police about the Christmas tree; China's voice floated down the hall, "No one remember anymore how it started."

China repeated, "No one gone say a word. I can guarantee that."

Unfamiliar guards walked the halls at night. Their faces were blunt, uncommunicative. They crouched behind their flashlights, peering into each cell, fear and suspicion in every move.

Glaring, the guards kept their cold beam on us long enough to make sure that we weren't dead. Shine it in our eyes, awake or asleep, watch us grimace, sit up in fear. Alive. Still locked up. Counted. They kept close watch to see if the supposed body moved or anything, a bit of flesh showing so it couldn't be just a bunch of pillows. "You never know with these women. As if they had nothing better to do but try escape."

The third day into the lock-down everything changed. We were pulled out of our cells, they said it was for showers. But in the shower room we were stripped, our clothes were searched, each seam hem zipper and fold. Looking for plastic explosives? They handcuffed us to the shower heads. "Spread 'em, squat, bounce. Bounce. Do it or get your stupid face smashed in, bitch."

Not easy to squat with your arms attached above your head.

No one got showers. The place stunk.

When it was our turn the bathroom was already noisy and full; Narcisse balked outside the bathroom doors, idiot eyes downcast, heels dug into the linoleum, she just didn't move forward any more. The strange guard hollered at her to move along, he grabbed her, pulled her around. I screamed at him, "She's deaf! She's deaf, you asshole!"

He stopped pulling at Narcisse, stared at me. "Oh hell. Tell her to go in there. She get a shower."

"No she won't."

Narcisse looked up at him, eyes blank and foolish as a

lamb while her clever long fingers unhooked the man's loosely attached handcuffs. We stepped into the over-crowded room, wriggling like eels deep into the crowd.

The guard went mad, actually foamed at the mouth a few minutes later when he missed the secure feel of the cuffs. Such small triumphs made our lives.

Swearing, the squad of goons began to tear each of our cells apart, stripping them to the bare bones: Bedding tossed into the hall, plants, coffee jars upended on top of that, books, diaries, letters, jewelry, clothing piled again on top. Televisions, radios pushed together in a jumble at one end of the hall.

They intended to put the terror back in the prison. Where it belonged.

We raved. Screamed. Our anger stank to the sky.

Time tough.

Looking at the wreckage of our cell we thought we'd lost everything. But, typical, in their shark frenzy they'd missed anything of importance: the radio and the con-traband VCR were gone, but my jar of hooch in the hop-per tank and Narcisse's stash in the false-back bookshelf survived the search.

Narcisse twinkled as she handed me a cup of tea, "Not knowing. Finding nothing."

"Typical," I signed. "Pigs is pigs." Narcisse wasn't the only one who could say it in Zen parables with her hands.

I unscrewed the upper portion of the metal bed frame and pulled out a couple of thin flexible pieces of steel, found the proper one to work the cuffs. "What in hell you going to do with these?"

"Dunno. Lock Johnson to the laundry sink?"

"Lock Rosalie to the cafeteria sinks?"

"Lock them together?"

The warmth spread up the back of our heads, we lay back on our stripped mattresses in our empty cell, checked out to another dreamland.

■   ■   ■

Sleeping was the first method of choice for doing time during lock-down. Unfortunately, screaming and banging on the cell doors were the second choices. The two factions were constantly at odds. Scream and sleep, bang and scream. Toss the damn hard-boiled egg back in the hall at the guards. What a life.

Then a little delegation of clean tidy people in unisex suits trotted down from the administration to interview us on the causes and instigators of the riot; they wanted names numbers places times crimes.

"Well, I didn't see anything, I was asleep on my cot all the time."

"You were seen out there, woman."

"No, man, not me. You know how we all look alike."

"We have sworn statements."

"Swore? Who swore? Just you tell me who swore."

"We need to talk, get this thing aired out."

"Right." Deuce handed them a list of grievances. "Everybody on this block thinks these here are some of the things we got to talk about."

The investigators were not pleased. "What? What?"

"These here. These here what we need to discuss."

When they got to our cell I told them that I would be happy to discuss the matter. From a legal point of view of course. First, we wanted a full disclosure of the prison's financial position.

The investigators didn't think that was within their jurisdiction.

"Well then, you got to do something about the medical treatment here, that damn hospital isn't even licensed!"

Voices battered at them from all sides, "We want some decent food, real doctors."

"Yeah. We want every sickening word from any hearing, what we said, what the officers said, how dumb the whole thing was, right there on paper."

This was not what the delegates had in mind.

I said, "We want legal counsel."

One of them glared at me. "Morgan, I've had about enough of this nonsense."

"Oh yes, sir. Me too."

Then Narcisse stood up, making the cell really crowded. She made throw-up faces, moved her thumb toward the door, stepped over to the toilet.

The tidy people made their uneasy exit, arguing among themselves. They carried Deuce's list with them.

A final voice echoed down the hall behind their departing rear ends demanding that all drugs be decriminalized, "Hell, we locked up already, what harm could it do?" There was a lot of support for that.

■   ■   ■

Rosalie was escorted up front. Cowboy wanted to have a little talk with her. She unlocked her teeth enough to give him a small wintery smile.

He asked her how she was doing, remarked that she looked a little pale.

She told him she damn well ought to look pale. "Nola's little bird got squished. Some pig just pinched its canary head flat. Bunch of savages working in this place. Don't talk to me about convicts." Big fat tears started up. "Who are these lunatics you have working here all of a sudden? Rapists. Fucking perverts. Throwing everyone's shit into the hall—bedding, clothes, everything. Killing little animals—worse than Old Norah."

He made placating noises. Felt sure she could see their point of view: "Don't forget that this prison is run on trust."

She raised a skeptical eyebrow.

"The events of the other day have caused everyone to have great difficulties."

"Great difficulties. I got your difficulties right between my legs. These guards are terrorists. That's what they are."

He sat on the edge of his desk building delicate designs out of paper clips. "My job is to get this place running again. I know that some of you ladies are thinking of causing trouble as soon as you're let out—"

Running the prison was not on her own list of priorities. "They're treating everyone like shit, even those of us who weren't involved at all." She tried to keep the whine out of her voice, changed it to a tremble at the last moment. She thought it would be effective.

He rode right over it. "I need your help to set things up so everything will run smoothly." Or would she prefer to do the next several years locked down under closed custody, only let out of the cell to work mornings scrubbing pots in the cafeteria?

He needed her help? Mmmm. "Who's running the place now anyway? Who are these creepy guards?"

"The warden has been relieved of her duties, a temporary acting warden has been assigned for the next several weeks."

"Who? You?"

He looked embarrassed. "Only until a permanent replacement can be found."

"No shit." Rosalie thought she could handle it. Maybe even profit from the situation. Sure.

• TWENTY–TWO •

"Was the night before Christmas and all through the prison,"

"Nothing was stirring and no one had risen."

"The junkies shot cottons with nothing to spare,"

("You guys work on this all week or what?")

"Anything to lighten our burden of care."

Thea's jaunty soprano broke in, "Ohhhh, fly me to the moon and let me geeze among the stars, let me see what junk is like on Jupiter and Mars! In other words . . ."

Gravel voiced, "Her-o-in, Her-o-in, with his band of men! Heroin! Heroin! He'll be back again!"

Lots of voices, "Steal from the riiiich—"

It broke down, half the voices for stealing from the poor too.

Claudia's voice, ragged, "Ladies! Ladies!" When no one paid attention she hollered, "Shut the fuck up, you goofballs!"

That worked. She took a breath. "You're going to be unlocked in awhile, one hall at a time, for one hour."

We made a joyful ungodly noise.

"For chrissake, don't blow it." Claudia stepped back into Control to pop the doors.

"Hey, Claudia sweetheart, c'mere, give us a kiss!"

"Cram it, you unlovely old whore."

We filled the hall with wild exultation, tangle of arms legs smiles hips lips thighs sighs, it was good to press flesh.

Claudia was smothered in the general embrace. Didn't seem to mind. I noticed Narcisse locked lip to hip with Deuce. They'd probably open a catering service.

China was nuzzling the back of my neck.

I liked it. "Where's Birdeye?"

She pulled me to one side, out of the crush. We leaned

against the wall. "They pulled her out of this block already—she on the short-time block now.

"No shit?"

"Another few days for the paperwork and she gone."

"No shit?" I was not holding up my end of the conversation.

China nodded, mournful. "I try to be glad for her, you know? But I'm going to be lonely." She lifted those magical eyes to me, shining like stars on a Christmas tree. "She got a date with the gate, you know I'm history."

Through the gate. It's like death or birth or something beyond our reach. I put my arm around her shoulder. "No shit." I wanted to be comforting.

Claudia stood on a chair at the mouth of the hall. "One more Christmas present, ladies: Officer Johnson has applied for an extended leave of absence."

"Praise Jeesus!"

"Make a joyful noise unto the Lord!"

Thea's fine soprano rose above the chatter pure and clear as a shot of crystal meth, soaring into "Silent Night." When the last tone faded she picked it up again, with "Sexual Healing"; we got through two verses before Cowboy, as acting warden, came down the hall, wished us Merry Christmas, told us all to lock in.

■   ■   ■

Narcisse and I were perhaps the only ones to see the prison's version of the Christmas spirit; it wasn't Saint Nick, it was Old Norah. The old rag doll was escorted out of the unit in the blue middle of the night murmuring, drooling and searching fumble-fingered through her pockets, dropping small items, whining for the guard to pick them up.

When they were at the last gate Norah began to scream, a thin high-pitched sound like fabric ripping.

"Serve the old bitch right get taken away, tortured: Half

her fault we locked down like this. If she hadn't gone bothering those weasel babies Lily woulda *been* gone well before Christmas the other year back."

"Now. That the truth."

After a day in the hospital out of her smelly cell Old Norah regained as complete possession of her faculties as she'd ever had. She decided it was time to make her will.

"Being of sound mind."

Those mad old bones.

She decided to donate her body to science.

"Free of all coercion."

They called me out of our cell to the hospital to write Norah's will.

Norah lay old old piss-stinking on a thin mattress, her wicked eyes darting around bright as two marbles, red lids bellied out below them. She would live forever.

She grabbed my hand with an unmuscled lock-bone grip, I couldn't pull away, sucked into the vortex of Norah's dying, a funnel a drain a suction pulling me in. Down.

Old Norah whispered, "I want to leave the money in my safety box to Lily." I tried to pull back. Her voice got stronger, "You think I have no humor?"

When I made out someone's will I put myself as executrix, so I get an automatic percentage of the estate. But being locked up made it difficult for me to see that all the points in a will were complied with. "Let's just get on with it. It doesn't matter what I think."

"Oh but it does. It does." Norah fumbled at the chain around her neck. "Here's the key to my safety deposit box." She pulled it back from my outstretched hand. "Just you wait, girl. You get it when I'm dead. You come get it before they cart my bones away. There's another ring of keys in my safety box. I give them to you. Yes." Norah nodded, a menacing grandmother kind of nod. "You know what to do with them."

She cackled.

I put Birdeye down as the executrix. I knew from humor. I glared at Norah. Keys? Cash? A big deal for nothing. Or something. Who the hell knew? A little fortune? What the hell was this business about keys anyway? Birdeye was going to have to find the safe deposit box for sure.

I had a sharp vision of those pre-med kids leaning over her cadaver. Studying the bones, the sinews, connective tissue, the unsouled detritus. Missing all the important details. Or perhaps not. Odd thought.

I finished it up as quickly as I could, uncomfortable under that mad old gaze, in a confrontation right at the edge of existence; I didn't care if her will made it through probate, cared even less about the fate of her corpse. Just rotten meat anyway. Damn.

"When's the old whore gone kick off?"

"Two packs say before we get out of lock-down."

"I'll match it, raise you one; says she ain't gone for another six months."

"She wait til Lily get back, you'll see."

"Left her a legacy—now, what it is, is what I want to know."

"We have to wait til Lily collect to find out."

"How she gone collect?"

■   ■   ■

The prison opened back up after the turn of the year.

Everyone wore a surprised look as if we'd been awakened from a long troubled sleep, a winter's hibernation. Stepping as if our muscles had shortened, as if we were unsure of our footing. Curious. Discovering not merely the extent of the actual world beyond our cells, but the resiliency of our own bodies.

There was a sharp edge to everything, a seeing as if for the first time, the abrupt shock of recognition. Places that grew legendary through the lock-down, the telling and the retelling, acquired a mythology which could not stand close inspection.

I wanted to see destruction. The damage was minimal. It rained for most of the lock-down, the black smudges on the brick already washed away; a couple of plastic couches, ripped and melted, hulked above the garbage in the morning fog like feeding dinosaurs. The rain brought delicate pale green patches of temporary grass back to life in the scorched yard.

It was the same old place. A grave disappointment.

There was no relief at being freed from the small confinements of the cell; quick and suspicious we took the measure of the larger space, tried to find an edge. There should have been some way to profit from all the energy we'd expended. Some slight movement forward, if not release.

Rosalie stood on the scale, groaning. Not a pound lost for all the weeks of virtual starvation. She determined to make up with Deuce, but was uncertain how to do it without getting killed. Deuce gave her that flat-eyed look of hers when they passed in the yard, Rosalie felt a trickle of sweat slide down her back. She still didn't know if it was sex or terror.

She'd made and unmade decisions just to keep in practice. Cowboy presented her with pretty clear choices, everyone but Rosalie knew that she'd go back up front. Which she did.

He mentioned Leonard only once. Rosalie thought she'd covered pretty well: "Oh that silly man. He's no one special to me, just a bus driver, used to drive the route I took to work. I thought it was nice of him to volunteer a visit." Big eyes innocent as a meadow. "I didn't know he was such an oddball."

Cowboy seemed mollified when she stepped close, leaned over his shoulder, murmuring that she was sure he would make a great warden even though he was far too smart to want the position permanently. It would age him prematurely. What was the point of all that pressure anyway? Enjoy the power now, step down out of the way when the heavy guns were brought up. They'd have even more fun after it was over.

She hoped like hell he believed her.

■   ■   ■

"It was," Alexander wrote me in a letter sometime in January, "a stroke of genius to have the police take Leonard's prints off my car."

The police were very glad they did so: Turned out he had a police record as long as his dick, was wanted on a parole violation. "Handy things, parole violations, made his prints easy to find. They want to question him about Roland's murder."

I could hear his proud voice through his handwriting.

"After checking out the prints the police seemed pretty confident that he was the one that did it."

Savoring his news, "I'm like a hero right now downtown."

I didn't think that was anything to spread around.

The envelope was postmarked from the Bahamas. No mention of the check Rosalie was supposed to have passed him.

His short conversation with Leonard had been awkward, he was embarrassed, he wrote, it seemed Leonard thought he was making a pass. Outside of getting Varney's phone number it originally seemed to have been an unproductive encounter. Then he thought to ask one of his police cronies dust the car, run the prints through the state computer.

Gratifying all around.

He tried to call Varney, but she'd already left town.

"In any case," he wrote, "China shouldn't be needing a lawyer anymore since the case will be closed by the time you get this."

Something wasn't right about that letter. I shoved my fist in my mouth, gnawed on the knuckle. My nose began to run. By all the indications I was having a nervous breakdown.

He wished me a Happy New Year.

• TWENTY–THREE •

Leonard was nervous, he didn't like visiting the prison, he'd had enough of prison. It should be the last time though, Rosalie set it up pretty well, it would go slick as owl shit. She'd said, just like Varney used to, "Oh yeaaah Leonard. Sure thing." She better be straight about it. He'd catered to everyone else's needs long enough.

He saw enemies on every corner, thought maybe he'd been followed, but soon it wouldn't matter, he'd be long gone. For now, he was cool. Working his game, totally cool.

He spun the usual tale of personal hardship, bravery. How he hadn't been done right. How faithful and considerate he'd been. "Going to send you in a piece last week, you know, but it didn't work out. I nearly got arrested just getting the cash together to come visit."

"Oh, Leonard. You shouldn't push yourself so hard."

"For you—of course I do. It's just us against the world."

He speed-rapped to Rosalie, "Damn I am glad you're not all bent out of shape. Some crazy guards around here. Takes a toll on a guy. After we do this check, split even, sure sure, then I think I should just mail you some bucks every month or so—keep you real comfortable, babe. After this run we'll cool for awhile, huh? You got the check?"

Rosalie stared at the table, fussing with the moisture ring the soda can left. She knew as she had always known that if she gave this man her check it would be gone. She didn't want to look at him. Hell, she was this total flop as a criminal, as a person. She wanted to smash the soda can in his face. She wanted to feel bones break. She bit her cheek so hard it bled.

The two men came into the visiting room wearing gray slacks, blue blazers, white shirts, conservative rayon ties. Their hair was cut well above the ears and collar, their nails were buffed, their leather shoes were polished. They looked bulky. Polite.

They approached the table smooth as snakes. The back of her neck began to tickle, the hairs rose on her forearms.

"Excuse me."

Leonard didn't even look up. "Hey. Buzz off, man. Me an my ol' lady here are having a private personal visit, you know?" His concern was directed toward Rosalie. As if he could smell the check in her belt.

"Sorry, buddy, but it's over."

Rosalie couldn't remember anything she'd done bad enough for these two horror movie creeps to come after her. She was too terrified to make a sound, her field of vision narrowed to a circle about six inches across focused on Leonard's face. Everything else went dark. She wondered if she was going to faint.

"Is your name Leonard Arthur Lee?"

He looked up at them, sullen, puzzled, recognizing only a new threat to his peace of mind, to his ever-elusive prosperity. He thought they were after Rosalie, maybe wanted him to witness something. They were going to bag the bitch behind something about the riot maybe— Damn, he hoped he'd be left out of it. "Yeah. Sure, man. So what?"

"I'm here to arrest you for the murder of Roland William Lee. Anything you say—"

Leonard stood up legs arms every which way, screaming, kicking over his chair, knocking into the nearby tables, looking for an exit. Spit collected ragged at the corners of his mouth, he cried out in all truth he never did that thing. China knows, China knows he didn't do it. Doesn't she. Doesn't she doesn't she doesn't she doesn't.

■   ■   ■

The next day Narcisse removed an official looking envelope from Alexander's box. Inside was one of China's missing checks, neatly countersigned by Rosalie. A second-rate maneuver. She was almost sweet in her naivete.

I taped it to the bottom of my desk drawer. Seventeen thou could be useful. Like insurance.

• TWENTY–FOUR •

I entered the visiting room about ten minutes after China, settling myself at a nearby table with one of the young lawyers eager for sisterhood. China's visitor had a mobile attractive face, a hungry mouth, burnished red hair.

Her voice was husky, tense, "Why is it that so many men talk a better fuck than they deliver? They look at me with those deep hungry eyes, murmur pagan love songs about how delicious my cunt will be, flick a tongue, roll me around for awhile, bang away with a loony grin, then grunting, collapse. Hell, China, I had to keep the pipe on the side table, got to find some satisfaction somewhere, you know?"

Sex and drugs sex and drugs. Thoughts bounced off the walls of my brain like neon: Varney. In the flesh. Smooth flesh.

She'd apparently run out of money wherever she'd been—seemed someone ripped her off. Slick.

China was very pale.

Varney chattered, uneasy, about how their real estate office had been transferred to the trusteeship of lawyers. "Not much different at first except that Roland wasn't around. I talked to the lawyers in triplicate. I took home fairly decent checks for awhile. We still handled a couple decent properties then, rental units, and the other." Shoulder lift, then drop.

Varney reminded China how horrified she'd been to hear China was accused of paying someone to kill Roland. China shrugged. Lift, drop.

Varney tried to change the subject, "Surprised that Leonard copped a plea to a manslaughter. Thought he'd fight it?"

China smiled, evil. "Not likely."

"Leonard didn't shoot him. You know that."

Casual, as if she hadn't heard, "Don't mind Leonard doin' the time, you know. About what he deserve. People all get what they deserve. Eventually."

"Umm. Roland was something too beautiful to live? Fragile? No. Not hardly." Varney chewed on a carmine nail, she broke through the barrier against the memory, the vision uncalled that came at his name, a ruined man broken splashed wasted gone unbelievable. Terrifying.

"It was a bloody mess. But I didn't shake. That came much later. The shaking, the crying, the fear of it. Right then the thing to do was get our money together."

China nodded. I was practically falling on the floor trying to hear.

Varney said that Leonard came in about then, began barking orders at her, so "I just sort of let him take charge, you know?"

China held Varney's hand so tight the knucklebones showed.

I thought I must be missing some vital point. It wasn't making sense.

My visitor inquired if I was feeling all right. I didn't bother to answer.

"Anybody around a dead man needs an alibi."

The police had pulled Varney in the next day, didn't like her story but she stuck to it. Some guy in a suit came in the little room, talked in that scary, important way they have, looking her over with those fish-eyes. They let her go. Good thing she didn't need an alibi.

She went home, she said, and Leonard had just gotten out of her shower, had a pipe all ready. She cried, he handed her the pipe and some line about the way to work out grief is through your body. She didn't remember what then.

Wishful thinking always played a large part in her relationships with men. It was just easier not to deal with their petty realities. As long as they did pretty much what she wanted of them—simple enough, just touch her, fuss over her, be eager to fuck her and charmed when she was coy, listen to her as if she were wise beyond their hope. Then when they slipped she'd give them a second chance, often a third. But after that of course, she was ruthless. Leonard was different. They had so much between them.

And Roland? Win a few lose a few.

China didn't relax her grip on Varney's hand. Their fingers should've grown together by then. "Go on, mija."

"I didn't know what to do—" Varney gulped, said she didn't want to discuss it any further. It was over. And over. And over.

"I got wasted at the funeral, you know that." Varney's voice quivered, "I already apologized to you for saying that even if the guy you hired didn't do it, it was someone else you paid to do the job."

"Stupid thing to say, eh?"

China finally noticed me hovering at her shoulder, dropped the conversation below my hearing level.

I said good-bye to the puzzled lawyer, went back to the law library. Perhaps a life of crime didn't suit me after all.

■　　■　　■

Soon after, Thea pushed her cart so it blocked the door into the library, brought me a jar. I poured myself a good one. "Thanks, here's to the success of the new distillery."

She nodded, too much understanding in her gaze. "Birdeye's legacy been keepin' us busy. Got you goin' too, hey, Morgan?"

I didn't bother to answer.

"When's Norah gone die so Birdeye will get some money?"

I poured again with a generous hand. "Don't know that there is money."

It does no good to spend a lot of time paying attention to the world we find ourselves in. The noise, the motion, the urgency of it all. For what?

Then China came into the law library, high heels click-ing, bracelets rattling, sweet deceptive lips smiling. She pushed some books off a chair, happened so often lately I didn't bother to pick them up anymore, she pulled up close, cooing at me, "You know that you can tell the length of a man's dick by the size of his wrist?"

She leaned over on my desk, peering into my face. "Hey, Morgan, you look awful. Pour me some of that?" She tapped my cup.

She smelled tropical. I poured with a judicious hand. Maybe it was just the smell of Thea's hooch.

Sipping, she mused, "Some people think they so slick. One dumb scam after another." She eyed me, cunning. "I wondered about Leonard being there with Roland dead, but Varney never mentioned it before. He musta shook the office down for the cash not realizing until later that it hadda be in checks—After awhile I didn't care who'd killed Roland, you know? Like you said to me, Morgan, finding the real killer isn't going to shorten my sentence by one day—"

"It's a matter of money."

Thea walked over to her cart. "Love to stay but I can't stand hearing about other people's money."

China waited until Thea was gone, then she said she wanted to kill all of them sometimes. It would have been so simple if they'd all worked together. But no. Snap. "Varney said that when Roland reached under the couch and brought out the sawed-off, she had no idea what was going on."

I thought I had an idea.

"Varney said she pushed at the gun, it wedged under his chin somehow. She said she'd hardly dared believe a shotgun could do so much damage, so irrevocable. She even touched him. You know, to see if he was dead."

China shivered her shoulders, they were wonderful shoulders.

"As if maybe he'd sit up, whistling that long low whistle he gave, they'd go on same as before."

"Awkward, him without a face."

She giggled. "Master fucking criminals. I'm the one ends up dangling at the end of a long long line of coincidences."

I knew I should be thinking faster. It was not easy. "You collected blood money though."

"Lost most all of it too." This was not quite the truth. "Well, a lot of it. Just now, Varney was sayin' she lost it all to some smooth lawyer dude in the Bahamas—"

"The Bahamas?"

"The Ba-ha-mas: beaches, expensive hotels, room service bellhops masseurs scuba divers muscle boys, the works." China rolled her eyes. "She was posing as a rich attractive young widow. Had some of my money with her, to invest, you know."

The men would be handsome gallant tender. Eventually they'd be supportive. The money they'd lifted off Roland was only enough to set it up. Varney was supposed to be sharp. "She thought a young lawyer come in useful, you know?"

I nodded.

"Well, when she got to the hotel there was this good-looking fellow, he was rich—young—sort of overwhelming, you know? She said he had a very cosmopolitan way about him."

"I'm sure he did." I had stuck Alexander's Bahamas stamp to my desk. Remind me not to be such a fool.

"Well, I don't know why you should have an attitude." China shook her hair out, petulant. "Wasn't you that got ripped off by your lover."

My stomach sucked up small but I poured with a steady hand.

"Which lover are we talking about now?"

China watched me with a small clever gleam, ignoring my dig. She rearranged herself, the picture of a pretty girl. "Seems the judge should reconsider my sentence now that Leonard's copped a manslaughter. I shouldn't have a conspiracy one."

"Different conspiracy."

"Roland's murder officially a manslaughter. That what the judge say."

"Thought we agreed that finding the real killer wouldn't shorten your time by one day? You didn't have nothin' to do with his murder so how come now you do?"

"Hey. I could be on my way out. Claudia says she'll escort me to the hearing if it works." She put her warm hand over mine. "I'd get some banking done."

I looked past her as I topped her drink off. Ignored her hand, her voice. "What hearing?"

"On my case. When you file an appeal." Smiling, she took my hand up, gentle. "I got an idea for a tattoo I could do for you, like a bracelet around here, no charge."

Her touch was electric. I ignored it. Thought of the check taped to the bottom of my drawer. Wondered if it would still be good when I got out. Wondered if it had ever been any good. "You got an idea wrong. What is it with this appeal all of a sudden? Now you think you beat me to the streets?"

"Oh nooo." She put her hand on my mouth, I licked her finger, bit it. She purred, "I don't go nowhere without you."

Ha.

"I thought I could maybe do a kind of dragon design for you, or one of those demons, you know, stretched around your wrist—"

Rosalie bustled in, saved me from responding.

"Hey you guys. How weird the thing with Leonard is. Did you think it'd be him?"

I got out a new pack of cigarettes, pulled a couple of the little lovelies out, lit two, passed one to China. "John Law got the wrong man. Again."

Rosalie looked puzzled. Uncomfortable. Left out, again.

I inhaled deeply. "How sweet it is."